bad boys

—Mick—

EVERYTHING'S NAUGHTIER AFTER DARK…

Book One

After Dark Series

D0841679

Melissa Foster

ISBN-13: 978-1-941480-40-3
ISBN-10: 1-941480-40-3

BAD BOYS AFTER DARK: MICK

Cover Design: Elizabeth Mackey Designs

WORLD LITERARY PRESS
PRINTED IN THE UNITED STATES OF AMERICA

A Note to Readers

My fans have been asking for a darker, sexier version of The Bradens (which are already super hot!), and I'm proud to bring you the Wild Boys and the Bad Boys in the new After Dark series. The After Dark series is written in the same raw, emotional voice as my other romance series, with naughtier language and amped-up heat levels.

If this is your first Melissa Foster book, you have a whole series of loyal, sexy, and wickedly naughty heroes and sexy, sassy heroines to catch up on with my Love in Bloom series (Snow Sisters, The Bradens, The Remingtons, Seaside Summers, The Ryders, and Harborside Nights). The characters from each series make appearances in future books.

Be sure to sign up for my newsletter so you never miss a release! http://www.melissafoster.com/newsletter

Complete Love in Bloom series:
http://www.melissafoster.com/LIB

For my readers

Chapter One

LURED BY THE pulse of sex and anonymity, Amanda Jenner moved through the dusky bar, brushing against silk, satin, cotton, and flesh, each graze feeding the adrenaline coursing through her veins. Blue lights misted over sweaty strangers lost in the seductive bump and grind of foreplay and hoping for a night of erotic pleasure. If Amanda tried hard enough, she could smell tomorrow's scent du jour—*regret*. Tonight she had no room for the confidence-crushing worry of what tomorrow would bring. She scanned the crowd, as she had in the previous three bars, immediately dismissing anyone who wasn't in costume. Her world was full of boring men who excelled at wining, dining, and boring her to sleep. Ten years of romance novels and movies had led her astray, sending her on a search for the elusive needle in a haystack. *She'd* led herself astray, always the careful thinker, careful dresser. Or as her younger sister, Ally, would say, *Careful kisser, careful lover*. Ally, however, had taken charge of her sex life—and she'd found the perfect man.

Now it's my turn.

Amanda was on the prowl, in search of a man who could wine and dine her, make her laugh, think, and feel—*for one night.* A man who not only knew how to get a woman off, but enjoyed doing it many times before taking his fill. If not for Ally, she wouldn't have known guys like that existed in real life. But now that she did, she wanted one, and the masquerade bar crawl was the perfect venue for her solo coming-out party.

Her eyes caught on the dark figure of a man, big and powerful, standing a few inches above the crowd. He leaned toward a woman wearing a slinky little black dress and a mask that covered her from nose to forehead, like Amanda's. Amanda's pulse quickened— for the broad, strapping, masked man, not for her competition. Like any good paralegal, she'd done her research, trading romance novels for *The Handbook: Release Your Inner Temptress* and stalking Internet sites for tips on flirting and taking charge of her sexuality. Then she'd practiced.

Excessively.

She'd spent weeks mentally role-playing her new vixen persona, using her boss, and secret crush of three years, as her prey. He was sex and sin all wrapped up in Armani and blessed with a beautifully smart brain—and off-limits. He never mixed business with pleasure, which made him the perfect fantasy playmate.

The masked man turned, giving Amanda a better view of his wide chest and shoulders, draped in black leather. *I'd like to be draped in you.* A shiver chased the thought. Was she really doing this? She inhaled a shaky breath and took in the silver mask dipping low on his cheeks, hiding some of his thick, sexy dark scruff, and riding up over his nose to his hairline. His gaze shifted, catching her staring. Her nipples tightened with awareness. The unfamiliar sensation startled her, momentarily shaking her confidence again. She averted her eyes to catch her breath, reminding herself this was what she was here for—a flash of fire, a forbidden fuck.

Pushing past the frightening thunder inside her chest, she curled her fingers around the hem of her treacherously short skirt. She couldn't chicken out. Not after weeks of research and pep talks. Especially not after finally finding the courage to get waxed from head to toe, including all the painful parts in between, which was easily as scary as standing in a crowd of strangers searching for someone to have meaningless sex with.

Oh God, am I really going to do this?

She chanced another peek at Leatherman, now casually leaning against a pillar and brazenly watching her. A dizzying mix of thrill and fear soared through her. She wasn't a quitter. Careful Amanda fought hard, but vixen Amanda thrust her aside. She was doing this. She was doing *him*.

If she could stop shaking like a frigging leaf. She lowered her chin, holding Leatherman's steady gaze. *One, two...I can't breathe...Three, four*...She tore her eyes away. Damn it. The book said to count to seven.

She'd build up. Practice on a few unsuspecting men before going in for *the kill*.

Kill? Really? That's awful.

Stop overthinking!

Inhaling a calming breath, she drew upon what

she'd read. *Chapter Fourteen, Conquering the Man of Your Dreams*, and knew what she had to do. Staring out at the sea of masked and painted faces, she conjured up her boss's handsome face and envisioned her tall, dark fantasy man moving across the dance floor, his attention trained on her.

He would never go to a bar crawl.

She sighed. *Not helpful.*

Her boss represented some of the wealthiest and most beautiful entertainers in the world. His female clients were always hitting on him or trying to set him up with their friends and sisters. That thought made her knees wobble even though it was known around the office that he never mixed business with pleasure, and she stumbled in her sky-high boots. She probably shouldn't have had two drinks at the last bar, but the liquid courage was necessary. Another masked man turned a predatory stare on her, his arm swooping around her waist as she tried to regain her footing.

His eyes slid over her face with little interest and dropped to the ample cleavage spilling out the top of her rib-crushing costume. *Perfect.* She swallowed hard to steady her mounting panic. *I can do this. The Handbook* claimed once the first seduction was under her belt, the rest would be easy. She wished she could skip the seduction part and go straight to the easy stage. Her brain told her to walk away. She didn't know this guy, or who he'd been with, or *anything.* But wasn't that exactly what tonight was about? Finding her sexual freedom? Owning it? She'd chosen the sexy black velvet dress with the tight bodice she could hardly breathe in and satin and lace trim that barely covered her ass specifically to throw off I'm-all-in vibes. And just in case that didn't say it all, she'd bought the lace-up fuck-me boots *Cosmo* suggested and the blond wig Bagyourman.com raved about—because everyone knew blondes had more fun.

Drawing from the flirtation tips she'd studied, she fingered the blond wig and drew in a deep breath, arched her back, and thrust her breasts forward.

The stranger licked his lips, and his eyes flicked up to hers long enough for him to say, "'Sup?" then slid south again.

Really? 'Sup? 'Sup wasn't a word. It wasn't even a greeting. It was a noise some lazy, uneducated person came up with because they couldn't put enough real words together to form a sentence. *I wore the outfit. I'm owning my sexuality. And this is who's attracted to me?* She could get this type of guy with hairy legs, flip-flops, and no makeup.

Ally's voice whispered through her mind. *You're doing it again.* Her sister claimed she limited her dating options by being overly judgmental. But Amanda didn't believe she was *overly* judgmental. She was smart. Period. Was it too much to expect intelligent conversation?

Her answer came in a recollection from *The Handbook*.

Chapter Three: Don't talk. Touch.

Right.

I can do without intelligent conversation for one night. Tonight she was uncorking her body and releasing her inner temptress. Acutely aware of the blazing bead Leatherman had on her from across the room, she flashed him her most seductive smile and turned the inferno he stoked on the numskull beside her.

"Hey." The word lingered on her tongue for a few

extra beats.

Genius took a swig of his beer, arm still fastened around her waist. "You're hot. What's your name?"

She wanted primal, and the only thing primal about this guy was his stench. Forcing herself to see him as foreplay for the main event, she said, "Lola," with practiced casualness. "You?"

"Rick." He nodded a few times, laughing under his breath.

She needed more alcohol for this. A lot more. "Buy me a drink?"

He peered over his shoulder at the crowded bar, giving Amanda an opportunity to scan the crowd for a different man to practice on, but Leatherman's gaze was too powerful to ignore, and it reeled her back in.

"Too long of a line," the man beside her said, and handed her his beer.

"Thanks, I'm good." She shook her head to tear her attention from the man she wanted and tried to slip back into character.

He tugged her closer with a lecherous grin. "I'm counting on you being better than good."

She closed her eyes briefly, trying like hell to bring on the fantasy so she could forget this guy was a stinky loser, but no matter how hard she tried to conjure up her boss's handsome face he refused to appear. Leatherman's stare drew her in like a slave. Adrenaline surged through her veins, a carnal ache growing low in her belly, filling her with pulsing heat.

This is primal. Her senses careened, and she fought the urge to jump up and down and scream, *I feel primal!* Frantically searching her mind for an escape from the man who had her in his grasp, she remembered chapter eighteen, *Gracefully Bowing Out,* and ran her fingers down Rick's arm, eyes still locked on Mr. You'll Do Perfectly for Tonight.

"Oh, I'm better than *good*," she promised. "But my friends are getting antsy. I'd better head over."

**

MICK BAD STRODE across the dance floor, sizing up the asshole gripping the blonde's arm. He'd come to the bar crawl hoping to get lost in a good fuck, and the blonde was sending the same greedy vibes, with an alluring hint of cat and mouse. He wasn't about to let this twentysomething shadow of a man get in his way. Mick had been that guy once, cocky and stupid, taking what he wanted despite the consequences. He'd carried the anger of losing his younger sister like a calling card for vengeance, but he'd outgrown that reckless troublemaking stage. Whoever said wisdom came with age was right. There were better ways to handle idiots like him. Unfortunately for this asshole, the anniversary of Mick's sister's death always brought him closer to the reckless edge, and if the guy pushed, he just might make an exception.

He stepped between the blonde and the man holding her captive, his six-three frame forcing enough space that the guy had to reach around him to keep hold of her.

"What the fuck, dude?"

Ignoring him, Mick put a hand on the blonde's elbow, and in his best disappointed-husband voice, he said, "Honey, I leave for a few minutes and you pick up another guy?"

"Wha...?" She turned from him to the jerk, who was spewing bullshit Mick also chose to ignore, and silenced as understanding dawned on her.

Mick gave her a reassuring nod, then turned to the guy. "Sorry, man." He draped an arm around the curvy blonde and strode away. She felt heavenly against him, well worth the moment of irritation.

"I was handling him," she said with a slight quiver in her voice.

"Thought I'd speed up the process. I can think of better ways to expend your energies."

"You can?" she said breathlessly. Her mouth snapped shut and she cleared her throat. "Can you?" she said in a more provocative tone.

Why he found that momentary innocence incredibly sexy was beyond him. He didn't usually go for women who were easily flustered, but he'd spotted her in the hotter-than-hell dress with the hint of white lace peeking out from beneath when he'd first arrived. Her attempts to hold his stare were impressive, and the enticing way she moved conflicted drastically with the nervous way she tugged at the hem of her skirt when she thought no one was watching. *An alluring combination of naughty and nice.*

Pressing his hand to her lower back, he brought her tight against his arousal.

"Absolutely," he promised. "Besides, you've been eye-fucking me all night."

She sucked in a ragged breath. "I..."

"Hey, no complaints here, and no pressure."

She reached up and touched his whiskers. It was a tender touch, not the rough stroke of a woman out to get laid, but behind her mask her eyes darkened. He lowered his face to hers and pressed a kiss to her cheek, testing the waters. He'd just taken her from the arms of an asshole. He shouldn't be thinking about all the dirty things he'd like to do to her so soon, but he couldn't deny the imploring look she was giving him, or ignore the feel of her soft, willing body. She spoke heady and low, talking under the noise of the bar instead of over it, and he wanted to hear more of it.

Unable to resist, he took her chin between his finger and thumb and angled her head up. "Let's take a test ride, see how we like it."

His mouth came coaxingly down over hers. She kissed tentatively, revealing inexperience that baffled him given her efforts at seduction. From across the room he'd been ready to bend her over the bar. Now he had the strange desire to keep kissing her. Chasing the unfamiliar and uncomfortable thought from his head, he intensified the kiss, taking her rougher and greedier. She returned his efforts with fervor, as if he'd untethered her. She moaned into his mouth, and it vibrated all the way to his cock. Holy hell. Had he been played? Was her tentativeness only a lure? Her hands locked around his neck, nails digging into his skin. He smiled against her mouth, happy to be her catch of the night.

Her body trembled as they feasted on each other's mouths, their bodies rocking and grinding to their own urgent beat. He maneuvered their entangled bodies to the edge of the dance floor, then into the darkness beyond, until her back met the wall.

"Don't stop," she pleaded.

Did she think he was a fool? No way was he stopping. He claimed her in another greedy kiss, eating up the sweet, sexy sounds leaving her lungs. He drew back, trapping her lower lip between his teeth and giving it a gentle tug as he mentally picked through their options. He was thirty-four years old and not exactly into having sex in a bar restroom, but his throbbing cock wasn't as picky. Behind her mask, her eyes were closed. He brushed his mouth over hers, placing a kiss to the swell of her upper lip.

"Don't stop," she repeated, stronger this time.

The hell with his distaste for bathrooms. He took her hand and pulled her down the narrow hallway toward the restrooms. She stumbled in her fuck-me boots. He gathered her against him and pushed through the men's room door.

"Out," he commanded to a guy who was washing his hands, and locked the door behind him.

He backed her up against the wall, kissing her hard and deep, exactly like he wanted to fuck her. Lifting her leg at the knee, he hitched it around his waist and rocked his cock against her. She tasted sweet, hot, and like the perfect remedy for his ghost-ridden week. Desperate to push past the painful memories, he shoved his other hand beneath her dress and tore her thong from her body, dropping the shredded material to the floor.

"Tell me to stop," he growled, hoping to hell she wouldn't.

She pressed her lips together and shook her head. The fluorescent bathroom lights sparkled off her mask and the glittery makeup caking her cheeks.

"I'm taking that as a green light. Is it a green light?" The attorney in him knew better than to assume.

She nodded.

"Thank fucking God."

He crashed his mouth over hers, kissing her hard and rough as he pushed his fingers into her tight heat. She moaned long and low, riding his hand as he devoured her mouth. She was so hot, so wet, he wanted to drop to his knees and consume her, but he was careful when he played this anonymous game, which wasn't often. Luckily, kissing her was like nothing he'd ever felt before. Her tongue was strong yet pillowy soft, and the deeper he delved, the more she gave, well worth the denial of tasting the sweetness between her legs. With his fingers, he furtively sought the spot that would shatter her world. She clawed at his arms, bowing off the wall with a loud, pleasure-filled groan.

"There. *There!*" she pleaded.

He slowed his efforts, drawing out her pleasure, and sealed his mouth over her neck, sucking, nipping, and licking, as she went up on her toes, her thighs rigid. He stroked his thumb over her swollen clit and her head fell back.

"Ohgodohgod—"

Her voice echoed off the bathroom walls as her sex pulsed around his fingers. He released the leg he'd been holding at his waist and she reached for the button on his pants. He grabbed her wrist and pinned it against the wall beside her head, still fucking her with his fingers, and brought his mouth to the swell of her heaving breast.

"Don't stop," she begged.

"I have no plans to stop until you have no more to give. You're going to come again for me like this, because I like hearing those noises you make." His voice was thick with desire, a husky command. "Then I'm going to bury myself balls deep and fuck you so I can hear it some more."

She trapped her lower lip between her teeth. The pained innocence of a sex kitten. His lips brushed over hers as he stroked the spot between her legs that made her body quiver against him. He took her in a slow, sensual kiss, and she surrendered to another intense climax.

"I bet your pussy tastes fucking sweet."

Her mouth gaped, and he brushed his thumb over her swollen lips. "You've got this innocent sexy thing down pat."

He kissed her again, ready for more. Lowering her hand from beside her head, he stopped cold at the sight of three freckles that formed a triangle between her thumb and index finger. His mind skidded to a halt. His chest constricted. He knew those freckles, had focused on them for the better part of three years.

In the space of a breath his lust-laden brain shifted the moment into some semblance of sense, which didn't make any sense at all. He looked at the eyes behind the mask, *really* looked at them, trying to piece together the blond hair and sexy outfit with the prim-and-proper paralegal he'd worked so fucking hard to resist.

"Will you fuck me now?" she whispered.

That innocence.

That voice.

Amanda.

He felt guilty, sick, and elated all at once. No wonder he was so drawn to her. *Fuck. Fuck, fuck, fuck.* What the hell was she doing at a place like this?

Did she know it was him?

He took a step back, his mind reeling. If she knew, she sure as hell wasn't letting on. And if she didn't, was he a complete asshole for not telling her right now? How could he? What if it embarrassed her? What if she had no clue and she turned it on him? *Sexual harassment? Fuck.* He'd fought his attraction to her every goddamn day. There were reasons he'd never crossed this line before.

He'd been three fingers deep inside her. He'd tasted her desire.

He was totally screwed and needed time to think.

"Hey," he said softly, not having any idea what was going to come out of his mouth as he righted her skirt and retrieved her shredded thong. "Fuck," he murmured under his breath, tossing the stringy material into the trash can. What had she been doing with that first guy? What kind of game was she playing?

"What's wrong?" she asked with a shaky voice. "What are you doing?"

God, Amanda. My Amanda. No. Definitely not my Amanda. He'd already crossed the line. He needed to tell her it was him behind the mask and costume. He gazed into her eyes. Heated innocence stared back at him, and his gut twisted.

He should tell her, but he couldn't. He fucking couldn't. He was too fucked to think straight.

"I'm, um..." *I'm never at a loss for words. What the hell?* He rubbed his chin, which reminded him that he hadn't shaved in days. His beard came in thick and black. Amanda had never seen him unshaven, and his mask covered nearly his whole face. There was a chance she hadn't recognized him. His mind spun again. If she didn't recognize him, what the fuck was she doing? Amanda didn't do things like this. She was as straitlaced as they came. Or at least she had been.

She *had* to know.

Was this her ruse to make a play for him? No. He hadn't been at work all week. She couldn't have known he'd be here tonight. But that thought was messed up, too, because Amanda didn't make *plays* for guys.

Only she *had*.

He was too confused to think straight, but the possibility of Amanda playing him had him stepping closer again, a smile tugging at his lips. He touched her glittery cheek, soaking in the curve of her face. He'd wanted to do that for so long, he had to grit his teeth to keep a moan from escaping.

He couldn't turn away. Not now. Not after he'd already crossed the line.

"Not like this," he said, shocked by the unbidden truth. "I want to do this right. With you in my bed, where I can savor you and pleasure you properly." What the hell was spewing from his mouth? He wanted her more than he wanted to breathe, but getting involved with Amanda went against the very morals and ethics he'd built his reputation on.

"Wh...?"

The hurt in her voice slayed him.

"I want you," he assured her. "Just not here. Not like this. This was—" *A mistake? Incredible? Wrong? So fucking hot I want to take you home with me right now?* He didn't know what it was, or what he should do next, but it turned out his mouth did. "Meet me tomorrow night. The Wine Garden, eight o'clock."

When she didn't respond, he kissed her again, tasting her sweetness anew.

Amanda.

He backed away, fearing he'd ask her to come home with him, and needing time and space to clear his head and think this through. This was a bad idea. A *very* bad idea. One that he was powerless to stop.

"Eight o'clock," he repeated.

She nodded. "The Wine Garden."

Taking one last long look, Mick opened the door, and the din of the bar rushed in. He placed a possessive hand on the small of her back, and they made their way out the front door. The brisk night air brought a modicum of clarity, and as they stood on the busy sidewalk, among throngs of masquerade bar crawlers, he observed her more closely. She nibbled on her lower lip, her eyes darting left and right, avoiding him completely. He'd kissed off her lipstick, but the thick rouge and glitter on her cheeks remained. There was no way he could have known it was her. Not in the dark, with the wig. Even now, with the bright lights of New York City shimmering off her mask, he struggled to reconcile the sex kitten before him with the Amanda he knew.

He hailed a cab, gave the driver fifty bucks, and held the door open for Amanda, unwilling to even think about her going back into that bar.

"Wait," she said urgently, one leg in the cab and one on the street. "What's your name?"

Holy Christ. She didn't know. She really didn't fucking know. Disappointment sliced through him, leaving a trail of confusion in its wake.

"I'm Lola," she said.

He let out a breath he hadn't realized he was holding. This must be part of her game, and he was happy to play along.

"Call me whatever you'd like, *Lola.*"

Chapter Two

"I TOTALLY GET it now, Ally." Amanda leaned across the café table the next afternoon, unable to suppress the foolish grin she'd been sporting since last night. "The thrill of the unknown. The power of knowing you're getting exactly what you want." Chills raced down her spine with the memory of what she'd done with the guy at the bar last night. She could still feel his big, strong hands touching and groping, his harsh, delicious kisses.

Her sister scowled and pointed her fork at her. "What you did last night isn't the same as what I used to do."

"What are you talking about? I followed all the rules in *The Handbook*. I waxed every nook and cranny, had a facial, used the best perfume, flirted like a pro...*almost*. I'm still working on that. But it worked! Two orgasms later, I've got a date with a mysterious guy who *definitely* knows how to please a woman."

She'd stayed up half the night reliving every

second, from the first bar she'd gone into to the drive home in the cab, and she'd gone from feeling exhilarated to regretful and explored every emotion in between. But none of the negative feelings stuck. She was too freaking proud of herself for not chickening out of her newest challenge. Maybe it wasn't the type of success she could tell their parents about, but she was proud of herself just the same. She'd pushed past her comfort zone and had a wild, crazy experience she'd never forget, and she wasn't about to let her sister rain on her temptress parade.

"A year ago I would have snubbed my nose at the very thought of going to a masquerade bar crawl. Check me out now," she said with a smug grin. "I'm *owning* it!"

"And yet here you sit in your flats and your sensible black skirt that hangs well below the knees, and you're buttoned up tighter than a nun." Ally shook her head and smiled. "You are *not* owning it. Besides, no book in the world can make you into something you're not. You know that."

"True, but it helps. It gave me the steps I needed, which, I'll remind you, baby sister, you never would."

"Still won't." Ally popped a forkful of salad in her mouth, clearly proud of herself. "It's wrong, Mandy. I mean, dressing sexier is one thing, but you don't have to pull out all the stops and have anonymous sex at night and then revert to Conservative Betty during the day."

"I'm *buttoned up* because of work. My boss isn't exactly the sex-it-up-in-the-office type. I swear, when I dress sexier, Mick barely speaks to me. Remember? I told you about that client meeting two weeks ago when he wouldn't even look at me." Amanda remembered it all too vividly. The muscles in his jaw had jumped during the entire two-hour meeting, and he'd made a point of *not* looking at her. He was clearly not impressed.

"Oh, please. You're gorgeous no matter what you wear, but when you reveal your hourglass figure, you resemble that redhead in *Who Framed Roger Rabbit*, only your hair is dark. He was probably sporting wood and couldn't think straight. But that doesn't matter. What matters is the dangerous game you're playing."

The thought of Mick getting hard over her was as exciting as it was ridiculous. The man never even gave a second look to his rich, gorgeous, and talented clients who unabashedly tried to seduce him. He didn't just draw a line between business and pleasure; he dug a gully. Not only that, but while Amanda considered herself a catch, he was clearly out of her league.

"You just compared me to a cartoon. Not exactly an ego boost." Amanda smiled, but while she could negate much of what her sister had said, the last part gave her pause. "Why is it dangerous? You did it."

"One, you wore a wig. Two, you used a fake name." Ally set her fork down and held up a finger for each point she made. "Three, you're seeing him again. Four, you got finger-fucked, not fucked. There is a difference."

Amanda's jaw dropped. "Wait, what? You said no names. *Ever*. How is that wrong? And it was masquerade night—what was I supposed to do? Go as myself?" More quietly, she added what she'd realized only a few hours ago. "And besides, in that wig, Al, I swear I'm a different person. Not completely. I mean I still had to give myself a few pep talks, but I felt pretty and sexy and..." *And the orgasms were out of this world.*

"Disguises bring empowerment," Ally agreed. "But you're seeing this guy again. What are you going to do? Wear a blond wig on your date and call yourself Lola? What is that?" She laughed.

Amanda's stomach sank. "Well, I *was*. Isn't that the game? And I could have gotten...*effed*, but he didn't want to do *that* in the bathroom. I think that's chivalrous, not dangerous. Maybe I didn't get"—she lowered her voice to a whisper, feeling like a Little Leaguer—"fucked." Then, in her normal voice, she said, "But it was fun and exciting, and he promised to savor every second tonight."

"With *Lola*," Ally pointed out. "What if you're having wild, passionate sex, the best sex of your life, and he pulls your wig off? What if it pisses him off? What if he gets violent for being played for a fool?"

Holy crap, she hadn't thought of that. "You think that could actually happen?" She'd have to go back and reread the section on *Leaving a Bad Boy* in *The Handbook*. There were great tips for getting out of sticky situations.

"Probably not, but there's always a chance. People are freaky." Ally reached across the table and touched her hand. "This isn't you, Mandy. You don't play games." She sat back, and her expression turned thoughtful. "I needed that control until I met Heath. Your personality is more giving, more lovingly submissive. You're better at letting someone else be in control, and that's not a bad thing. I think men prefer that, actually. When you first told me what you wanted to do, you said you were doing it to attract more exciting men. You've done that. You know you can do it. I think you should let it go and go back to being yourself."

Ally had met her fiancé, Dr. Heath Wild, at a medical convention where she'd been volunteering. What started as a one-night stand had turned to all-consuming love. Amanda had never seen her sister more centered or happier. Was it wrong for her to want the same?

She'd always told Ally the truth, and what she'd said had been honest, but there was more to it, and now, seeing the worried expression on her sister's face, she swallowed her pride and came clean.

"I can't. Not yet. You're so happy with Heath, and I'm truly thrilled for you, but I'm so jealous I can't see straight."

"Mandy," Ally said with the type of deep understanding that could only come from a sister and best friend. "You'll find the right guy, but not this way. Whoever this guy is you're meeting tonight, he's not going to be *the one*."

Considering I can never have the one I really want, that's a reasonable assumption. Mick had been out of the office all week. She loved her job regardless, but when he was in the office it was that much better. She respected him as an attorney and admired him for his strong moral compass. Weaker men would have taken the gorgeous women who propositioned him without giving it a second thought. But beyond his kindness and legal skills, he was fiercely loyal to his family, which amped up his sexy factor tenfold. He was always meeting one of his three brothers for lunch and thought nothing of excusing himself from meetings to take a call from his mother.

"I have no hopes of tonight's date being *the one*," she said honestly. "I just want a night of great sex.

That's it. No more."

Ally squinted curiously. "And you're meeting him at the Wine Garden?"

"So?"

"I don't know. Just don't go back to *his* place. Or *your* place. That's dangerous no matter how he wines and dines you. This whole thing—seeing him again, the wig, the *game*—feels like it's riddled with trouble. If you're dead set on sleeping with him, go to a hotel, and make sure you make yourself memorable when you check in. Maybe Heath and I should show up, just in case."

"Ally, I don't need a babysitter."

"Seriously. We don't need to sit with you, but that way we can identify the guy."

"Ohmygod. You've already got me killed?" She sighed. "If that were his plan, wouldn't he have *effed* me and killed me last night in the bathroom? There's no way he'd have gotten caught; there were too many unidentifiable people in masks and makeup. I'm telling you, his entire face was mask and beard. I can't wait to see him without his mask. I wonder what he *really* looks like."

"Yeah, I wasn't going to say anything about the abrasions above your lip."

Amanda covered her mouth, her lips tingling with the memory of their toe-curling kisses. "I tried to cover it."

"Use Neosporin before you go to bed, and keep makeup off of it." Ally crossed her arms and smiled. "And I can't believe I'm giving you advice about whisker burn. If he's any good, your thighs are going to burn, too."

"From his whiskers?" A tingle of excitement

darted through her.

"Among other things. Your stupid book should have told you to start working out three months before your little temptress transformation. And for what it's worth, any man who really falls for you is going to fall for the real *you*—flats and all."

She'd met those men, and that was exactly why she couldn't be herself.

**

MICK HADN'T BEEN worth a damn all day, having spent half the night beating himself up about Amanda and the other half scouring his firm's employee handbook and operating agreements. There was nothing about interoffice dating, which made things even more complicated. He had no easy, legal out. The decision was fully resting in his usually capable hands. But for the first time in his life, those hands felt subpar for the job. He *wanted* Amanda. He'd wanted her for too damn long to make it easy to walk away. And now that he'd had a taste of her, now that he'd seen the side of her he'd denied himself, he wanted *more*. If she'd been anyone else, he could walk away. He always had. *Give, take, leave.* Easy, clean, unencumbered. Nothing lasted forever. The death of his sister and the demise of his parents' marriage had proven that, along with a million other shitty things that came along with relationships.

Despite what Amanda had done last night, he knew she wasn't the type of girl who hooked up with random men. She was too smart and too good of a person for that. She was the type of girl a man married and cared for. Hell, she attended romance novel readings like others attended church.

Why do I know that?

He was worse off than he'd thought, and he could never offer Amanda what she deserved. He didn't *do* relationships, and he sure as hell didn't plan on doing marriage and children. Watching his family fall apart was hard enough. He had no interest in setting himself up for the gut-crushing pain his family had gone through.

He really needed to come clean and then walk away. Set last night aside as a mistake. *An incredibly wonderful mistake.* He'd mastered the art of gracefully turning down advances from his eager and beautiful clients, yet here he was, walking into the Wine Garden, about to cross another line with Amanda.

Mick strode through the quaint bar, ignoring heated glances from hungry women and seriously questioning his judgment for the first time in his adult life. His eyes drifted from one table to the next, seeking the only woman he wanted and fighting against the battle ensuing in his mind. Spotting a gorgeous blonde sitting at a table in the back of the bar, nervously fidgeting with her napkin, his heart raced with recognition. Weren't they well past this ruse of disguises? He slowed, taking advantage while unnoticed to drink her in. Her plunging neckline revealed the swell of her breasts. Heat stroked down his spine with the memory of feeling her frantic heartbeat against his tongue when he'd tasted the silky swells.

She raised her head, and her brows knitted with confusion.

Holy hell. She had no clue it had been him last night. The realization hit him in the solar plexus like a bullet train. She'd been ready to fuck a stranger in the bathroom of the bar. His hands fisted by his sides. His gut knotted and burned. He was surprisingly turned on and pissed off in equal measure, which made no sense, because he had no right to be pissed off. He'd screwed plenty of strangers, and Amanda wasn't his to claim. But she was *not* the type of woman a guy fucked and forgot. Hell, she wasn't the type of woman a guy *spoke to* and forgot.

He closed the distance between them slowly, allowing her time to make the connection.

"Mick? Wh-what are you doing here?" Her eyes darted toward the front of the bar.

"I have a date," he said more casually than he felt. "What's with the wig?"

She touched the wig as if she'd forgotten she had it on. "I...um." She paused as he lowered himself into the chair beside her. "It's a joke," she said in a shaky voice. "You can't stay. I'm meeting someone."

"Are you?" He sat back, taking in her high cheekbones and her slim upturned nose. He'd always found her beautiful and preferred her natural beauty to tonight's vixenish makeup. But that didn't mean he didn't appreciate the seductively dark shade of red on her full lips—lips he was currently picturing wrapped around his cock.

"Tell me about him," he urged. If she wanted to play, there was no game he couldn't master.

Her big, round eyes darted around the bar, their innocence belying her sultry makeup. "He's..." Her gaze finally landed on him, and he felt his lips curve up in a *go ahead, tell me* smile. She scanned the front of the bar again, then her eyes returned to him, serious and confused.

She pushed to her feet, wobbling on a pair of black spiked heels as she reached for her purse. "He's late. Probably stood me up. Oh well. I guess I'll see you next week."

Mick rose to his feet in front of her. Her floral scent permeated his senses, but his mind replaced it with the arousing scent of her desire from last night. His cock twitched with the memory, and he searched her face for a sign of the same recognition. Beyond her confusion, there was definitely something provocative and eager trying to remain hidden, but it wasn't the clarity he was looking for, and he hated knowing it wasn't meant for him—at least not knowingly so.

With a hand on her elbow, he guided her to the chair beside him. "Stay."

"But your date?"

Holding her confused gaze, he shifted in his chair, bringing his knee between her legs. Her breathing hitched with the intimate move. She blinked several times. He was as drawn to her innocence as he was to her daring prowess. Lifting her hand to his lips, he kissed the three freckles that had given her away last night, watching as her confusion deepened.

"Mick...?"

"My date is already here." He leaned closer and whispered, "So is yours, *Lola*."

**

THE RICH, SEDUCTIVE sound of Mick saying Amanda's fake name skated through her befuddled brain, wreaking havoc with her ability to think clearly. He was touching her in ways that sent shocks of heat to her core—and sparks of confusion to her nonfunctioning brain. His leg brushed against her inner thigh. He held her wrist—*like he did last night*. She was riveted in place by his piercing stare as he watched her with faultless calm, trying to make sense of her boss and the mysterious masked man being one and the same. A bead of sweat formed between her breasts. Her heart slammed against her ribs. She swallowed hard, thinking of all the dirty things they'd done, the things he'd said. *I bet your pussy tastes fucking sweet.*

Oh God, what have I done?

Mortified and stupidly thrilled, she turned away, catching sight of blond hair moving with her, driving her embarrassment up to shoot-me-now level. She couldn't believe she'd felt empowered in the stupid wig. Why hadn't she listened to Ally? She wished she could snap her fingers and disappear. Mick didn't like when she *dressed* sexy—and last night she'd gone full-on slut. Plus, here she sat in spiked heels and a whorish dress she'd bought after work with the sole intent of seducing her mystery man. She must appear foolish and immature.

"Mick, I..." *I'm an idiot.* She eyed the door, wishing she could run out and never look back. Her lower lip trembled with a painful mix of anger and embarrassment. Not only did she not have a mystery man, but now she needed to quit her job. How could she ever face him again? She rose on shaky legs, but his hand on her wrist kept her near.

"Sit down, Amanda. Please." His tone was careful, purposeful, his stare unwavering and commanding, and somehow also warm and inviting.

She sat down and crossed her legs, feeling exposed. Ally was right. She wasn't *owning* any of this.

Forcing herself to be brave, she studied him, putting the pieces of his face to the man last night. She saw it now, his eyes behind the silver mask. His face beneath that jet-black beard. But wait. He *knew*?

Anger climbed over her embarrassment, shoving it down beneath the regret, beneath the fear of losing her job, making her shake all over. "Why didn't you tell me it was you?"

"I didn't know," he said with the same calm he might use to offer coffee.

This didn't make any sense. She'd never known Mick to lie, which was one of the things she respected most about him. But now she wondered how well she knew him at all. The unflappable professional who didn't like her to don sexy attire had been out for a fast fuck in a seedy bar? She shouldn't be surprised that he would hook up with a random woman in a bar, but she was. It *floored* her.

There was only one way for her to survive this conversation. She drew her shoulders back and told herself she was discussing work, not staring at the man she'd fantasized about and seduced. *And come for—twice.* Not the man she'd thought was pure gentleman but turned out to be as animalistic as...*as the type of man I was seeking.*

Gulp! Okay, time to pull my shit together. She forced herself to sound confident. "Then you must be really disappointed to have found me sitting here."

"No, Amanda. It's not like that." He ran a hand through his thick hair, still holding her wrist like she might bolt—which she was seriously considering.

Lowering her chin, she leveled him with her best don't-even-try-to-lie stare. He'd taught it to her, and she'd mastered it for interviewing clients and witnesses.

"Tell me, Mick. What *is* it like?"

"I didn't know when I saw you in the bar," he said in a low, firm voice, holding her gaze. "And I didn't know when we were in the bathroom." He slid his hand from her wrist to her fingers, curled his big hand around them, and stroked the skin between her finger and thumb. "I realized it at the end, when I stopped. When I saw this."

She followed his eyes to her hand. She wore no jewelry, and she had no idea what he was referring to. "My hand?"

"Your freckles." He brushed his thumb over three freckles between her thumb and index finger.

Knowing the man she'd been crushing on for years noticed something so small made her feel special, though she knew it probably shouldn't. "You noticed my freckles? On my hand?"

"I happen to have an affinity for them."

"For freckles?" This had to be a come-on. An outright lie. Something to take the bite out of the fact he'd brought her to orgasm last night and promised so much more for tonight without revealing his true identity.

"No." He leaned closer and slid his hand along the nape of her neck. She melted a little despite her warring thoughts. "*Your* freckles. Like these." He brushed his thumb just below and behind her ear. "When you wear your hair in a bun, I can see those."

I have freckles there? She'd died and gone to heaven.

No, this wasn't heaven. It was hell. He'd been at the bar for the same thing she was last night, but it obviously hadn't been his first time. He held her other hand and ran his fingers along the length of her arm, sending prickles of heat to her core.

That feels really, really good.

Tapping his finger on the back of her arm, he said, "And the four you have here."

His gaze was serenely compelling. He was no longer looking at her like he was trying to figure her out or bring them both up to speed. It was confusing her, making her feel more vulnerable and...*wanted.*

"Mick...?" *What is this? What are you doing?* The questions lodged beneath disbelief.

"That's why I stopped." He sat back, leaving her feeling bereft. "I realized it was you."

He was the man she'd pined for, her forbidden fruit, and he was making her feel warm and mushy. She couldn't afford to be warm and mushy. Her job, her reputation, *and* her sanity were on the line. She had to keep this in perspective and remember why he'd been there last night. He was good at the game she'd only dipped her toes into. This had to be part of that game for him, not the baring of his true emotions she was twisting it into.

"But you would have gone through with it with anyone else," she challenged.

"As would you." His voice was dead calm, nonjudgmental.

She turned away, embarrassment creeping back to the forefront. *Own it. Right.* She was clearly not made for the temptress life if she couldn't tell one man from another. She forced herself to face him again.

"I stopped because it was *you*," he repeated. "I wanted to do this right."

Right? What did that mean? That he wanted *her* and not just any woman? Or that he was following through with a promise? This was supposed to be a night of anonymous sex. Sleeping with her boss was not part of her game plan—and having sex to fulfill a promise he made when she was still in the dark about his identity *wasn't* happening.

"Well," she said, her back rigid. "This isn't what I'd planned. Not by a long shot."

"What did you plan, Amanda?"

How could she admit the truth? To *him*! It didn't help that he already knew exactly why she was there. What was the alternative? Make up an even lamer excuse? She needed help.

"I need to go to the ladies' room." Grabbing her purse, she rose to her feet, but he snatched her hand, holding her stare for a long, painfully silent moment. She was sure he could hear the blood rushing through her ears.

"Don't take off on me." The stern command conflicted with the tender kiss on the back of her hand that followed.

It took all of her focus to get to the ladies' room without stumbling. She had no idea what game he was playing now. Was this payback for last night? Would he sleep with her and then fire her? Was it a control thing? Did he want to have sex with her so every time she saw him in the office she'd have an even better understanding of who was boss—in the boardroom or the bedroom? She pushed through the ladies' room doors and plunked her purse down on the counter. She looked at her trembling hand, wondering what all that stuff about her freckles really meant. She dug *The Handbook* from her purse, frantically flipping the pages until she found what she was searching for.

Remaining in Control. She skimmed the chapter,

feeling like she was on a game show and up for the ten-million-dollar question. Only this was no television show, and the prize was sex with a man she wanted—*desperately.*

She read aloud to hear over her thundering heart. "Picture the man you want to conquer." *No problem there.* "Now picture him naked and tied to a chair." She slammed the book closed. *Mick naked and bound to a chair?* Not helpful. She'd felt his impressive cock last night, and the thought of it there for the taking...

Oh God.

How was he sitting out there so calm and in control when she was falling apart at the seams?

She was so far out of her league she couldn't even see the field. She considered calling Ally. She would know what to do. But that was the problem, wasn't it? She knew her sister would tell her not to even entertain whatever was going on out there, but to walk right out the front door. But as scared and confused as she was, Amanda's heart was wrapped up in that man, and she didn't want to turn her back without knowing if anything he'd said was true.

She caught a glimpse of herself in the mirror. No, not herself. *Lola.* Blondes did not have more fun. Blondes apparently got into sticky situations with their bosses. Ally was right. Again. She hated that. *Amanda* was usually the *right* sister. She was a skilled paralegal; she wasn't a woman who hid or cowered. She wasn't pitiful. And she sure as hell was not going to allow her boss to see her as such.

The hell with this. I am owning this transformation once and for all. She removed her wig and began brushing out her dark hair. *Right here, right now.* Her spine of steel righted itself one brush stroke after the next. *Regardless of the consequences.* Okay, that part kicked her in the back of the knees, because the consequences were high, and she cared about them— her job, her reputation.

She spent the next few minutes giving herself a pep talk, preparing to look Mick in the eye and own up to what she was doing last night *and* what she'd planned for tonight. If he could have sex with a stranger without guilt or regret, so could she.

Feeling jealous of a fictitious stranger, she shoved the book in her purse and began her pep talk once again.

Chapter Three

AMANDA MOVED CONFIDENTLY across the dimly lit bar, her dark eyes trained on Mick, chin lifted proudly. He found her renewed confidence insanely hot, but regardless of how badly Mick wanted her, he knew if he allowed himself to feast on the remarkable woman heading his way even for one night, it couldn't end well for either of them. His mind reeled back to the first day they'd met, the day she'd interviewed for the paralegal job. She'd worn a conservative blue suit, a white blouse buttoned up to her neck with a strand of baby pearls around the collar, a pair of sensible heels, and a confident expression. But her trembling fingers and the way she'd shifted in her seat told of her underlying nerves. She was fiercely determined and graceful in her presentation—an enticing combination of tigress and gazelle.

She'd come a long way since then, smarter, savvier, but she'd never hardened like other women. He was glad to see she'd ditched the wig. Amanda didn't need to *be* anyone else. She was enough—more than enough.

Her straight dark hair framed her beautiful face and spilled over her shoulders. He'd fantasized so often about how her hair would feel trailing over his bare chest, he could practically feel it sweeping over his skin now. He recalled the feel of her soft curves molding to his hard body last night, the sexy sounds she'd made as she'd surrendered to their passion. Fire coursed through his veins just thinking about how close he'd come to being buried inside her.

One night. He needed one night with her. Then she would be out of his system and they'd have no unfinished business. He nearly had himself convinced of it as she took her seat beside him, her shoulders squared, face serious.

"I ordered you a sidecar." He pushed the glass across the table, knowing there was no way in hell he was going to leave without her by his side.

For a second her wide eyes gave away her surprise, but she checked that emotion quickly. "Thank you. How did you know I liked them?"

"Just a guess." He didn't like to lie, especially to Amanda, but the truth would have given him away. There wasn't much about Amanda he hadn't noticed. But he'd been careful to keep his feelings at bay during the long nights they worked together after hours, and in all the daylight hours in between. "You look exquisite. I'm glad you lost the wig."

She nodded, a hint of a smile curving the edges of her mouth. A flush rose on her cheeks. "You don't like it when I dress sexy," she said matter-of-factly. "So please don't pretend otherwise."

"I don't like..." He shook his head, sure he'd heard

her wrong. "I don't like what?"

"Please, Mick. Don't patronize me," she said sharply. "I get it. I have a professional image to uphold. But other girls in the office wear higher heels and low-cut blouses."

He didn't give a damn what any of the other women in the office wore as long as they dressed professionally enough to uphold the firm's image. But hell if he wanted Amanda's knockout figure on display for every other man to admire. He'd given her the wrong impression entirely, but he didn't want to talk about work. That was a troubling subject he'd rather not think about, much less talk about.

"We're not at work," he reminded her, hoping to sway the conversation away from the topic.

She took a drink, impressively meeting his steady observation. "You asked me what I had planned tonight."

"I did." He wanted to reach for her hand, to tell her it was okay, that she could trust him, despite the fact that he should be telling her the exact opposite. He was intrigued by this darker side of her, and he wondered if he'd spent three years thinking she was someone she wasn't, or if this was something new.

She lifted her chin ever so slightly. Anyone else would probably have missed it, but Mick was determined not to miss a thing.

"I went to the bar crawl last night intent on seducing a man. And I came tonight with the same purpose. I'm not embarrassed by it. I'm just not that good at it yet."

Holy hell. Not good at it? She was very good at it. Then again, he was attracted to her vulnerabilities, which other men might have been turned off by, like the death grip she had on the glass, which he knew was to still her trembling hand. He liked when she'd slipped into a voice full of breathless wonder and the way she'd asked if he was going to fuck her in a tone that sounded like she wasn't sure if she was using the right words.

"I think you're quite good at it," he said honestly.

Her eyes narrowed, and she smiled. He knew this smile well. It was the *you think you've bullshitted me* smile, which she used very effectively when they were meeting with clients.

"That's kind of you, Mick," she said without the confidence her expression conveyed. "I know I have a long way to go." Her brows knitted again. "But I'm going to get this right."

The tigress and gazelle were in full play. Could she be any more adorable? Going to get it *right*? He took a long pull of his drink—his second drink, having downed one when she was in the ladies' room.

"With who? Some scumbag who'll take advantage of you?" His protective urges surged forward. He'd had trouble keeping them in check when it came to Amanda these last few months. In fact, he realized, he'd been having trouble since she'd started with the firm.

"No." She sat up a little straighter. "*I'm* going to take advantage of *them*."

Over his dead body. "Why?"

She cocked her head. "You tell me. Why do you do it?"

Boy, he'd taught her well, hadn't he? He couldn't tell her the truth—because he wanted no part of a relationship. Because love wasn't real. Because nothing lasted forever and he wasn't about to open himself up to that sort of pain. Because shit happened that he couldn't control and, at some point, life would make him into a liar. So he went with the next best thing. A portion of the truth.

"Intrigue. Excitement. No strings to complicate things."

She nodded. "Me too."

"So you've done this before?" She was hot, smart, and she'd gone on plenty of dates, but the thought of her hooking up with a random guy made his skin crawl. Thank God he'd been there last night.

"Well, no, but—"

He let out a breath he hadn't realized he was holding and struggled to keep his emotions in check. "Why, Amanda? Why do you want to seduce a stranger? And don't regurgitate my answers, because we both know it's a cop-out."

She ran her finger nervously along the edge of the table, her face softening.

"You go on plenty of dates," he reminded her. "With respectable guys. Lawyers. Businessmen."

His eyes found hers again, big and round and gut-wrenchingly innocent. "You're gorgeous and smart. You could have any number of men. You don't have to reduce yourself to that."

"Reduce myself? Is that what you were doing last night? Reducing yourself?"

"No. Yes. I don't know." He finished his drink, wishing he'd had a few dozen more. "Not with you, but when I hook up with random women? Yes, I guess I am. It's filling a void. Don't you see that? I don't do it often. It's been a particularly difficult week for me, and last night was my attempt to forget."

"Forget?" Her voice filled with curious

compassion.

She was too bighearted to jump to conclusions. If he'd told any other woman he wanted to get laid in order to *forget*, they'd assume he meant to forget another woman. Amanda's brain didn't work with the same insecurities. Or at least that's what he'd thought before last night. Her need to seduce a stranger had to be bred of insecurity, didn't it? As far as he knew, she had no torrid past.

He needed a clear head, and bringing up the reason for his tumultuous week would only make things worse, so he tried to steer the conversation back on track.

"This isn't about me. It's about you."

"Fine," she said sharply. "You want to know the truth?"

He cocked a brow. She knew he dealt in truths, save for the little white lie about her drink.

"I can't believe I'm even considering telling you this," she said softly.

She smiled and he was glad to see her genuine, easy smile. The smile that took no effort, unlike everything else she'd done tonight.

"I'm a boring-man magnet. The guys I attract might be businessmen, but they're duller than concrete. I'm just trying to change things up. To find my inner sexy. To learn to flirt and seduce like other women do. To learn how to attract edgier men with better personalities and..."

"And?"

"And...God, Mick. You're my *boss*. You don't need to know all of this."

He shifted in his seat, guiding her knees between his, and placed his hands on her outer thighs, watching her carefully. Her eyes widened. The pulse at the base of her neck quickened, pleasing him greatly.

"I was three fingers deep in you last night. I made you come twice. I don't *need* to know, Amanda. I *want* to know."

Before she could respond, he lowered his voice and ran his fingers through the ends of her hair, just above her breast, enjoying the quickening of her breath.

"What are you looking for? An anonymous sexual adventure? A hard fuck to break you out of your conservative shell?" He moved his hand to the base of her neck and ran his finger along the dip at the center of her collarbone. She drew in a sharp breath.

"I happen to be very attracted to your conservative shell, but if you want someone to break you out of it, come home with me tonight." He paused, letting his words sink in and reluctantly reminding himself one night was all he could have. *One. Night.* "I'll give you the fuck of your life, with a man you know and trust. I'll keep you safe, you'll get what you crave, and no one will ever know."

"I can't. You're my...Mick?" She was trembling again, the good kind of trembling.

"Tonight I'm not your boss, Amanda. Tonight I'm your stranger." He slid his hand over the top of her thigh, grazing his fingertips along the crease just beside her sex. "One night of pleasure. A fantasy. No strings. No regrets." He brushed his lips over hers and pressed a kiss to the corner of her mouth. "Just one night, and we'll never speak of it again."

AMANDA MUST HAVE lost her mind. That was the only reasonable explanation for why she was walking into Mick's penthouse apartment, allowing him to slide her purse from her shoulder and press a kiss to the base of her neck. And her collarbone. And her jaw. At some point she'd closed her eyes, because when he stopped kissing her, she opened them and found him gazing at her with that look again. The one that made her feel desired and sexy, despite her pinging nerves.

His lips curved up in a sinful smile that made her heart race, and he dropped a hand to the small of her back, guiding her further into his spacious apartment.

Toward our night of debauchery.

Oh Lord.

Her boots broke the silence, tapping a slow beat on the hardwood floors. Moonlight spilled in through two enormous round windows on the far wall, filling the room with an erotic bluish hue. A large island separated the kitchen from the living room, and two columns framed a glass elevator beside an open staircase. *An elevator?* Her entire apartment could fit in one quarter of his first floor.

"Your apartment is gorgeous."

"You're gorgeous; *it's* functional," he said casually, leading her to a fully stocked bar by one of the round windows.

Her head was spinning. He was really good at this. So good at it she might need to drink an entire bottle of liquor just to forget how she paled in comparison.

"Functional?" she said nervously. "Mick, you have an elevator."

He poured them each a drink. "We'll make good

use of that elevator." He stepped closer, their bodies brushing from hips to knees. "And the bedroom, and the crow's nest."

Her body burned with anticipation. *Crow's nest?* Was that a kinky position she didn't know about?

"And the bath," he promised in a low voice, pulling her tight against him.

She heard a whimpering sound and realized it came from *her*.

He pressed a kiss beside her ear and whispered, "And the staircase."

He dipped his finger into his drink and dragged it along her lower lip, then followed it with his tongue. Her knees weakened and she grabbed hold of him to remain standing. She was still trying to imagine what they would do on the staircase and he was already six steps ahead.

"Shall I go on?"

"Mick. I...I'm totally out of my league with you," she regretfully admitted.

He set his drink down and wrapped his arms around her waist. "You're here. You *are* my league."

"But all those things you said. I don't, I haven't..." How could she say this without sounding like a total loser? "I'm still learning. I can't even imagine what we'd do on the stairs."

He ran a finger down her cheek, under her lower lip, and held her jaw between his index finger and thumb. *Kiss me. Please kiss me.* He dragged a finger over her lower lip, pushing it just far enough into her mouth to touch her tongue with the tip. The slow, precise move made her damp.

"You want this, Amanda." He slid his other hand to her ass and squeezed.

Yes.

"I'll show you everything you want to know." He pressed his cheek to hers, reminding her of the jet-black scruff he'd sported last night.

"Your beard," slipped out before she could stop it. "You didn't shave last night. You always shave. That was another reason I didn't recognize you. Your beard was thick, like you hadn't shaved in days."

"I hadn't. But I shaved this morning. For our date." He touched his lips to the abrasion above her upper lip. "It grows fast. I'll shave again if it's too harsh for you."

"No," she said quickly. "I like it. I just didn't recognize you with it *and* the mask."

"Then it stays."

His voice was better than rich milk chocolate, better than a warm summer afternoon, better than...*anything.* He lowered his mouth to her neck, placing openmouthed kisses from one shoulder to the other. Each kiss brought a pulse of pleasure. She closed her eyes and tipped her head back, giving him better access and hoping he wouldn't stop this tantalizing awakening of her senses. He grazed his teeth over her jaw and nibbled his way to the nape of her neck, where he lingered, placing kiss after delicious kiss. She'd dreamed of this moment, but nothing came close to feeling his strong hands around her, his hard body—and it was *hard*—against her, or his glorious mouth taking and giving pleasure in equal measure.

"Those freckles. I love those freckles." He pressed another kiss to the ones below her ear and framed her face with his hands. "Open your eyes."

His command was as thrilling as his touch, and the

dark look in his eyes stoked the fire burning inside her.

"When you wear your hair up, I want to bend you over my desk and take you from behind, just so I can see those sweet little marks that belong only to you."

"Wow." The awe-filled exclamation sailed from her lips unbidden, and she clamped her mouth shut. "Sorry. I didn't mean to say that. I just..." *Really want you to do that.* Oh, man, she was losing it. "You're really good at this."

His eyes narrowed. "*This?*"

Making me fall for you. One night was all this would ever be. She needed to remember that and assure him she understood it. She'd remember this night for the rest of her life, unless she screwed it up and he sent her home, which she had a feeling she was on the verge of doing.

"Seduction," she explained. "You know, the whole game of it. That's what I need to learn."

"Fuck," he mumbled, confusing her again. "Right. The game. Well, don't use that line, because that was just for you."

"The freckle thing?" God, she loved the freckle thing, but surely he didn't mean it the way she took it, like he *really* meant it. "I know. Thank you."

He touched her face again, and his electric gaze sent currents coursing all the way to her toes. She would be perfectly happy staying right there in his arms, doing nothing more than gazing into his entrancing eyes. Nothing would ever measure up to this magnificent moment she'd somehow lucked into—and secretly, selfishly twisted into more than she should.

He laced their fingers together at her sides and

brought them behind her back as he moved forward, trapping her between the bar and his strong frame. His eyes turned suddenly serious, darker, boring into her, stroking her from the inside out. How did he do that?

"If I do anything you don't like, or anything that makes you uncomfortable, tell me to stop."

Anticipation stole her voice. She nodded and mouthed, *Okay.*

"Trust me?"

"Yes," she whispered. *I always have.*

"Good. I'd never hurt you." He pressed his lips to hers. "We should talk about the important things up front, to avoid it later." He kissed her again. "Condoms, always use them."

Oh God. More embarrassing talk? "I do, but I'm also on the pill."

"Good," he said more sternly. "You can't trust guys to tell you the truth when it comes to sex." The muscle in his jaw jumped, like he hated telling her that.

"But you just asked if I trusted you. Was that a trick question?"

He made a sexy groaning sound that vibrated through his chest to hers. "When you tell me things that way—"

Oh no! She was already screwing up? "What way?"

"With wide eyes and that sexy, innocent voice. It kills me. It makes me want to stop talking and carry you upstairs."

"Isn't that a good thing?" She smiled, proud of herself for doing something right naturally, without having to try.

"Christ, Amanda."

Oh boy, the look in his eyes was tortured and hot

at once. This was new. This, she loved.

"It's a very good thing. But this is serious. You can trust me. You know me. I'll never lie to you. But other guys? They want to get laid, and it sucks to wear condoms, so they'll tell you they've always used them just to get you to say you're on the pill and forgo using them."

His tone was caring, firm, and pained at once, and it touched her deeply.

"They want to fuck you, feel you, and forget you," he said coldly.

His words stung, but she knew he didn't mean them to.

He brushed the back of his fingers down her cheek, and his tone softened. "But you can't put yourself at risk like that."

"I know about diseases. I'm not a child."

"I know. But this isn't just a game, Amanda. You can get hurt in so many ways. I need to be sure you know what you're getting yourself into."

She hadn't expected him to do more than give her a night of hot sex, but she probably should have known he'd be careful, make sure she understood the ground rules. Because when she'd first started working with him, he'd spent many long evenings meticulously going over things he said other attorneys and paralegals overlooked, to ensure she was as careful as he was.

"Thank you for caring enough to want me to be protected."

"Baby, if something happens to you, I'd have to go out and find a new paralegal."

Baby. Her heart squeezed even though he'd made a joke. She reminded herself to keep this light and went up on her toes, pressing a kiss to the center of his chin. "So romantic."

His eyes narrowed and he wrapped one hand around both her wrists, holding them behind her back and kissing the center of her breastbone. "Does that hurt?"

"No." She closed her eyes, reveling in his strength and his tenderness as he kissed the swell of her right breast.

"Lesson number two." He dipped his tongue into her cleavage, then blew on her damp skin, bringing goose bumps to her flesh. "There's no place for romance where hookups are concerned."

"Ever?" That surprised her. Couldn't a hookup also be romantic?

He used his other hand to unzip her dress and slid it off one shoulder, pressing a kiss to the skin he bared. "If a guy gets romantic, you're not hooking up. End of story."

Using his teeth, he slid the dress from her other shoulder. The silky material hitched just above her elbows and beneath her breasts, revealing her black lace demi bra. She was breathing so hard she half expected him to tell her to chill out.

"So beautiful," he said, eyes locked on her breasts. He ran his finger just above her bra with a feathery touch, sending chills through her. "I have an affinity for black lace."

He lowered his head, placing hot licks and long, sucking kisses, over the same path. Her nipples hardened, and she arched against his mouth, aching to touch him. She struggled to free her hands, but he held her captive, every mind-numbing touch stealing more of her brain cells. She closed her eyes and moaned as he sealed his mouth over her nipple, sucking and stroking her through the lace.

She felt a whimper rising from her lungs and didn't even try to resist it.

"Love the sounds you make, the way you taste," he whispered, before moving to her other breast and giving it the same scintillating attention.

She told herself what he said shouldn't sound romantic, but it felt like a lie. He released her wrists, and her dress slipped to the floor, leaving her bare save for her bra and heels. She closed her eyes against a wave of embarrassment.

His lips touched hers lightly, a tease of a kiss. "Open your eyes." His voice carried the command smoothly to her ear, beckoning her in the most seductive way.

She opened her eyes, and his lips curved up in a gratified smile.

"Lesson number three. Watch. Always watch." Passion blazed in his smoldering stare as he placed his hand between her legs, cupping her sex. "Waxed bare. So fucking sexy."

He didn't move, but his dirty talk and the tease of his fingers against her wet skin made her sex clench.

His eyes darkened. "So ready for me, baby. I like you needy. I can't wait to feel you do that around my cock." She felt her entire body flush. He pressed his lips to her cheek and said, "Don't be embarrassed. This is what you're here for."

She didn't respond. Couldn't. Could barely breathe. Her thoughts about learning how to seduce ebbed as he slid one finger between her wet lips, stroking her slowly and ever so lightly. She mewed and rocked, urging his finger inside her, but he resisted, teasing her, taunting with his thick finger until her legs were numb. Her brain replayed one thought over and over: *More. More.* She might have even said the words; she wasn't sure, couldn't think to save her life. She grabbed hold of his arms in an effort to remain erect. His thumb moved circles over her most sensitive nerves, sending ripples of heat down each numb leg to the soles of her feet.

He lowered his mouth to hers, brushing their lips together. "Your pussy is so wet. So fucking sweet. Tonight you're going to come on my mouth."

The naughtiness of his words brought another flash of heat and a low moan that sounded carnal and dark. She never realized dirty talk could have such a powerful effect or be so addicting. She wanted more. She wanted it all.

He kissed her hungrily, rough and tender at the same time. His tongue thrust into and searched her mouth, while his fingers played to their own slow beat, driving her up, up, *up*. She arched against his hand, wanting more, needing more. But he had his own agenda and slowed the kiss, turning it sensual, languid, prolonging the exquisite torture.

"I could kiss you all night." His breath was hot against her skin.

That's definitely romantic. Isn't it? They obviously had very different views of romance. Either that or her brain was too befuddled to process anything at all. She had no idea how he could talk. Her entire being was liquid heat. That didn't seem to matter, because he took her in another perfect kiss that sent sparks straight to her core. She moaned loud and needy, and she didn't care, because his touch, his mouth, his voice, were sheer bliss. He unhooked her bra, freeing her breasts, and sucked her nipple—*hard*.

"Ohgod, Mick—"

He made a male, primal sound of gratification so full of lust it propelled her closer to the edge. He sucked harder, to the point of pain. She closed her eyes as the sharpness seared through her to exactly where she needed it most. He *finally* pushed his fingers inside her, and she couldn't stop the sounds of pleasure streaming from her lips. He sucked her breast and fucked her with his hand, stroking the same glorious spot time and time again. An orgasm swelled deep inside her, building, pounding, clawing for release, stealing her vision from the outside in. She dug her fingers into his waist, his arms, wherever she could find purchase as her body fought to reach the pinnacle, bucking and jerking in sweet anguish.

"Don't stop. Please don't stop." She'd never felt such immense pleasure. It radiated up her center, spiraling outward as the climax gripped her core, burning, aching, tingling, until it enveloped every inch of her, and she cried out again.

"My name, baby. I want to hear it."

His harsh command intensified her pleasure. "Yes. Mick—"

His mouth crashed over hers, urgent and demanding as she surrendered to the crest, riding his hand, arching every part of her body. Craving more, more, *more*. He was right there with her, knowing exactly what she needed. His fingers slowed, moving in and out, stroking her clit with lethal precision, taking her right up to the edge until she spiraled over again. She tore her mouth away, wanting to give him what he'd asked for.

"Mick—" His name tasted like heaven and sin as

she surrendered to the titillating pleasures.

He sucked her tongue into his mouth, mimicking the rhythm of his fingers. The eroticism of it sent her body convulsing again, taking and taking all that he had to give. She hung in the heightened state for what seemed like forever, but in reality was probably only minutes. As her climax eased, he kissed her more tenderly, staying with her again, through the very last pulse. He swept her into his arms. She felt drugged and boneless—and safe, so blessedly safe—against his muscular chest.

He pressed a kiss to her forehead. "I've got you, baby."

Nestled in his arms, she knew she'd never be able to *just* gaze into his eyes again. Nothing would ever be the same. Nothing would ever be enough.

Chapter Four

AMANDA BLINKED UP at Mick from within his arms with a combination of innocence and sensuality that made his chest tighten. A sweet smile curved her swollen lips.

He'd kissed her too hard, and though he shouldn't let it, it pained him. He'd be more careful with her, or at least he'd try. Mick wasn't an *I've got you, baby* type of guy. He was a taker, a *leave before daylight* type of guy. He'd never allowed himself to care about a woman before, but he'd cared about Amanda for the better part of three years. She was smart and beautiful, trusting and kind. She deserved a real relationship with a man who didn't know the harsh realities that life held. But the thought of any other man touching her sent fire through his veins— sparking more dangerous emotions. Emotions he'd had to fight hard to quell when he'd warned her about what to watch out for with other men. But he'd had to do that, too, because as badly as he wanted to claim

Amanda as his own, he knew he couldn't. And that was killing him.

She sighed, and he lowered his lips to her, drinking her in.

He'd been just fine before last night. For years he'd buried his feelings beneath lust and carnal desires, pushing them deeper with every meaningless hookup. But all it took was a few hours with Amanda to unsettle his carefully erected walls. Now he struggled to put things back in the untouchable compartments where they belonged. It was torture trying to shove them back into the cold abyss, but he had to do it. He'd already broken one of his long-standing rules of mixing business with pleasure. Actually, he'd broken two. He didn't bring women to his apartment, and yet here she was, in his arms no less. Her skin was flushed and warm, glistening with the sheen of a satisfied lover, and they'd only just begun. He'd promised her a night of unbelievable sex, and that's exactly what he intended to give her. One night to satiate years of desire. One unfuckingbelievable night they'd never forget.

Time to get his mind back where it belonged. *In the game.*

He lifted Amanda to the bar, placing her hands on the rounded edge of the glossy wood. He stood between her legs. Her expression was serene, making him want to pull her back into his arms. *Not happening.* Not if he had any chance of keeping perspective. He pushed her legs apart, probably too roughly, but that was for his sake as much as hers. She sucked in a sharp breath, her eyes wide.

"Wake up, baby," he commanded, leaving no room for contemplation. "It's time to feed your man." He pulled her to the edge of the bar, regretting his choice of words. *Baby? Your man?* He really needed to get a grip.

And he did. On her *ass,* as he lowered his mouth between her legs and took his first real taste of her desire, slicking his tongue slowly along the seam of her glistening sex. She moaned, and the sweet, sexy sound sent lightning to his groin, earning a throbbing complaint from his cock. His cock wanted in on the game, but it would have to wait. His emotions were still too close to the surface. If he buried himself deep inside her now, he'd have no hope of holding back the emotions still clutching his heart. He stroked his tongue up her center again, loving the way she rocked her hips. He knew what she wanted, but he wasn't in a hurry. One night was all he'd get, and he intended to enjoy it. He kissed her cleanly waxed skin, moving over and around her center. The heady scent of her desire was intoxicating, like the pleas streaming from her lips—"More! Mick! Please!"—but teasing was half the fun, and the feel of her muscles contracting against his tongue was fucking amazing.

She grabbed his head, trying to direct him. "Please," she pleaded.

That's it, baby. Beg for it. With his hands beneath her ass, he lifted, bringing her to sit on the very edge of the bar, and unfurled her fingers from around the wood. He guided her hands behind her, so she was leaning on her palms, legs spread wide. *Fucking perfect.* Wonder and want shimmered in her eyes, battling for focus. He splayed his large hands over her trembling thighs and pressed them open wide. Three freckles formed a straight line on her right upper thigh. His fucked-up brain wanted to see those pretty little marks as a sign that they were meant to be together, but that was a chick thing to do. *And totally messed up.* He shoved that thought away, replacing it with the only thing that would help him remain distant—greed.

Amanda panted with anticipation. Her sex twitched and glistened for *him*.

"Mick," she pleaded.

"Feel the need coursing through you? That's for *me*, Amanda. When you're with some other guy"—his gut twisted and burned—"you're going to think of this moment. You're going to think of me. You're going to *wish* it was me." He held her there, bared to him, soaking in the *for him* part, allowing it to brand into her brain.

"Don't say that about some other guy." Her eyes filled with sadness, and it nearly took him to his knees, but she needed to hear it. *He* needed to say it.

"One night, Amanda. That's all this is. All it can ever be. Never to be spoken of again." He gritted his teeth against the anger that clarification brought. "Still with me?"

She inhaled a shaky breath, the sadness in her eyes pushed lower by determination. Seeing that determination messed with his head.

"Yes," she said with an unwavering stare.

He placed one tender kiss to the sweet marks on her inner thigh, then tightened his grip on her legs and gave in to the inferno burning inside him. He devoured her, licking, sucking, and tongue-fucking her into a writhing, jerking, wet, needy mess of pleas and moans. He sucked her swollen clit, grazed his teeth over the sensitive flesh, and thrust two fingers into her tight heat. Stroking and sucking until her hips bucked off the bar and she screamed his name. He withdrew his fingers midorgasm, replacing them with his mouth, and moved his finger to her ass, playing over her tightest hole and keeping her at the peak. She moaned and arched, pushing against his finger.

"Don't stop—" she pleaded.

He'd intended only to tease her, but the allure of taking her everywhere was too much, and he pushed his finger past the tight rim of muscles.

"Ohgod Mick!" Her head fell back with another cry.

Her ass was tight and her pussy was soaked, both clenching with every inward motion. He used his other hand to unfasten his pants and quickly stepped out of them. While eating at her center and finger-fucking her ass, he gripped the base of his cock, fighting the urge to bury himself balls deep, and squeezed the root to slow his release. She screamed his name into the dark room, her body convulsing in jerky snaps. He stayed with her, fucking and thrusting, sucking and stroking, until she fell limply to the bar, panting. A fucking fantasy come true.

It took everything Mick had to fight the urge to hold her, to confess the emotions she roused. He moved around the bar, eyes on the sink as he washed his hands, forcing himself to regain a shred of emotional distance. He stripped off his shirt and tossed it aside. It was time for flesh-to-flesh contact.

**

AS AMANDA CAME back down from the clouds, the sting of what Mick had said about other guys filtered back in. He'd sounded callous and cold, but what they were doing felt intimate, like it was more than just hot sex. She knew that was her unrequited feelings taking over, and she had to stop allowing them to.

She was supposed to be practicing seduction techniques, but his every touch turned her mind to mush, making it hard to think about doing anything other than giving herself over to him and soaking in the pleasures he expertly doled out. She'd never opened herself up to any man the way she was to Mick, and something told her she never would. But it was exactly that line of thinking she needed to stop. She pushed herself up to a sitting position, determined not to become like the harem of female clients clawing for his attention. This was her one night with the man of her dreams, and damn it, she wasn't about to screw it up. *No more emotions.*

He came around the bar, bringing his glorious— *Naked? When did that happen*—body into full view. Her mouth went dry. She clamped her jaw tight, and embarrassingly, she gawked. His eyes gleamed like volcanic rock. His lips curved up in a wicked smile that told her he wasn't nearly done with her yet. His beautifully sculpted biceps bulged as he lifted her from the bar and lowered her feet to the floor, watching her intently. She was supposed to be seducing him, learning, trying out the techniques she'd studied. Her eyes moved slowly over his tanned, muscular chest and powerful, broad shoulders. They drifted further south to perfectly sculpted abs that led to—*hello*—the most perfect penis she'd ever seen. Not that she'd seen that many, but it was smooth and thick, reaching past his belly button, so tempting she was salivating. So much for her dry mouth.

She stepped closer on shaky legs. His eyes bored into her like lasers as her fingers played over his chest, and she pressed a kiss to his nipple. He made a deep, appreciative sound in his throat, spurring her on. She did it again, and his cock jumped against her skin. Empowered by his response, she kissed his other nipple and laved her tongue over the pebbled peak, earning another eager bounce of his shaft. That was all she needed to give in to the seduction and allow her mouth to take over. She kissed his pecs, between them, under them, over them, her mind spinning with desire. Every kiss, every groan he uttered made her wetter and more confident. Mick was breathing hard, but his hands remained at his sides, his fingers curling and uncurling like he was itching to touch her. She didn't need to look to feel his heated gaze.

Watch. Always watch. A thrill chased the memory of his words.

She blazed a path down the center of his abs, letting her hand drift between his legs and cup his balls.

"Fuck," he hissed.

She released him, her eyes darting up. "Too hard?"

He guided her hand back to his sac. "No, baby, just unexpected."

Baby. Her heart squeezed, and she reminded herself it was just what he said in the heat of passion. He probably called all of his women *baby*. She closed her eyes against a wave of sadness and focused on the feel of his hard abs against her lips, his heavy sac in her hands, and the intensity of his breathing. Moving her other hand over his muscular thigh and around his hip, she gripped his ass. His hips pistoned forward, and he groaned again. A smile tipped her lips. She kissed the hard plane of flesh between his hips. His cock bumped her chest, hard, hot, and tempting. He gathered her hair in his hand, and she met his wolfish stare. She swallowed the nervous fear tugging at her and sank lower. She was five six, and he was over six feet, which meant she'd be in an odd bent-over angle if she wanted to taste him. She eyed the stairs, and without a word, because she knew she was way past being able to speak, she took his hand and guided him over. He sat down, knees wide, a lascivious grin on his lips.

She knelt two steps beneath him and pushed her hands up his thighs. There wasn't a shred of fat on him, and his perfect cock stood straight and rigid, eagerly awaiting her next move. It should be illegal to look as sinful as he did. And she should probably worry about her not-nearly-perfect body, or what she was about to do, but the way he was staring at her made her believe she was just as hot as him and sent her worries away. He fisted his hand in her hair as he'd done earlier, watching as she lowered her mouth. Just as she got her lips around the broad head, he yanked her up.

"Ow!" *What the hell?*

"I'm sorry." He caressed her scalp, his eyes full of regret and something more. Before she could decipher it, he pulled her face to his and kissed her deeply. He tasted of her, and she desperately wanted to taste of him. When their lips parted, he held her so close she smelled the scent of her desire on his breath.

"Listen to me." He sounded angry, but his eyes told her he'd shifted into protective mode again. "I'm clean, but other guys..."

She wrinkled her brow in confusion. "No blow jobs? But..."

"It's risky. You need to know."

"But you just had your mouth all over me."

"You said you'd only had protected sex. Guys lie, baby."

The endearment softened his warning. "Are *you* lying? About being clean?"

"No. I told you I'd never lie to you." He gritted his teeth again, then touched his forehead to hers and closed his eyes. It was the single most touching thing he could have done as he dragged her emotions all over creation.

"Christ, Amanda. I feel this need to make sure you know these things, and it's messing with my head. I know it was...*inconvenient* to stop you when I did, but I have to know you're going to be safe."

He used such a caring tone, conflicting with the struggle to restrain himself written all over his face, but she knew, like everything else, she shouldn't read too much into it. He cared about her as a person, and maybe as an employee, but that was as far as it went. This was a night of sex. Nothing more.

And it was his turn to be pampered.

"Okay. I promise I'll be careful." She gently pushed his chest, and he leaned back on his elbows, his chin set low, his eyes hungrily watching her.

She ran her hands over his thighs, stroking the length of them, watching the reaction of his cock as it bobbed against him. Taking a hint from his playbook, she spread his legs wider, holding them there as she dragged her tongue over his sac and felt it tighten against her tongue. He groaned with pleasure, thrilling her to no end. She'd given a blow job before, but it was a very long time ago, and she'd never experimented below. She wanted to experience everything with Mick. She cupped his sac, fondling as she licked his sensitive skin. She made a point to keep her eyes trained on his. Watching him watching her, seeing the restraint and desire warring in his features filled her with the power of control. She dragged her tongue from base to tip along his hard length, repeating the move until he was panting, his muscles corded tight. She wrapped her fingers around his cock and swirled her tongue over the broad head, laving and teasing his sensitive glans.

"Fuck," he hissed. "That's good, baby, so good."

The compliment gave her the courage she needed to lower her mouth over his shaft and take him in deep, withdrawing slowly, letting her mouth acclimate to his girth and length. Her hand followed her mouth in tight strokes up and down his cock, ending each with a swirl of her tongue along the tip. She felt him swell impossibly thicker and knew he was close. She wanted to taste him, to know she'd given him as much pleasure as he'd given her. He sat up, tangled his hands in her hair, and guided her at a faster pace. She sucked harder, squeezed his cock tighter, shocked by her own eagerness to make him come in her mouth. Suddenly he tugged her head back and crashed his mouth over hers, kissing her hard. So fucking hard she felt it between her legs. But this was *her* turn. *Her* seduction, and she wasn't done.

She tore her mouth away, and confusion filled his eyes. She wasn't about to back down. He'd taken what he wanted—not that she was complaining—and she wanted the same. She wanted to *take*. "I want this."

"Baby, you don't have to go all the way. It's okay. I'll come later."

"I..." The tenderness and heat in his eyes drew the embarrassing truth. "I've never let a guy...I've never..."

Panic spread through her with the thought of leaving and not having done this with him, because after Mick...? She was so busy telling herself not to go there, she couldn't even *think* about after him.

"I know we only have tonight," she assured him. "And we both might regret it tomorrow, but I want to do this, and I want to do it with you."

"I'll never regret tonight. We said no regrets." He touched her cheek, and she leaned in to it, soaking him in.

"I know. No regrets." *Except that it is only one night. How can I not regret that?*

He closed his eyes for a beat, and when he opened them his expression was warm and tender and hot and hungry at once. "Are you sure?"

"Yes."

He searched her eyes with a soulful expression. She wondered if he saw the emotions she was trying to hold back, or if her nerves shadowed everything else. She didn't really want to know the answer, and pressed her lips to his to snap out of the thought, then lowered her mouth to him again. He held her hair back but didn't guide her this time. She began as she had before, teasing, slicking her tongue along his hard length, licking his sac, fondling and stroking as she took him in deep. He smelled musky and safe, and for this one night, he smelled like he was hers.

"You feel so good, baby. So fucking good."

She moved faster, took him deeper. The head of his cock banged against the back of her throat, and she remembered what she'd read about relaxing her throat. She tried, but her mouth was stretched so wide it was hard to concentrate and still keep her rhythm. The hell with thinking. She let her desires guide her, and guide her they did. She worked him with her hands and mouth, and he groaned and rocked and made noises that made her ache for his touch. As if he'd read her mind, he leaned forward, slightly to the side, giving her space to continue her pursuit of his pleasure, and ran his hand down her ribs and between her legs. She moaned around his cock.

"Christ, that felt good," he said in a gravelly voice.

She moaned again, and his hips bucked. She rode his hand in time to each stroke of his cock as he teased her magical spot. She sucked harder, moaning with pleasure against his erection as his fingers pushed into her and a torrent of pleasure consumed her. His cock swelled, his muscles flexed, and hot jets of salty come pulsed down her throat. She struggled to breathe, gulping down his release as storms of heat tore through her, scorched her limbs, pulling at her core, engulfing her very being with the same dark possession as Mick owned her heart.

Chapter Five

AMANDA SAT TWO steps below Mick with her cheek resting on his thigh, eyes closed, her lips slick with his essence. She'd sucked his cock like she owned it, given him a mind-numbing orgasm while in the throes of her own, and she was completely and utterly fucking with his head. They still hadn't consummated their night of sex, and he felt the emotional doors he'd welded closed rattling at the hinges.

He lifted her into his arms, cradling her against his chest and trying to ignore the way his insides softened with her sigh of surrender as she snuggled against him.

She reached up with a sated smile and touched his cheek. "Mm. Your beard comes in fast."

He didn't respond because the more she spoke, the harder it was to remain emotionally distant. He was fucked and there was only one way to get unfucked—with an icy exterior. But he'd tried that before they'd moved to the stairs, and all it had taken was a flash of her doe eyes and a single word in her breathless voice to dial him right back up to an emotionally possessed inferno.

He carried her upstairs and stopped at the threshold of his bedroom. Why was he here again? Why hadn't he taken her on the couch, where it would be easier to get her to leave afterward?

Because I'm fucked.

Determined not to be, he turned, intent on retreating to the first floor. The closer to the door the better.

Amanda touched his cheek again, gazing up with eyes full of trust and something else he couldn't read but felt in that dark place he was trying to ignore. Hell if he didn't turn around and carry her to his bed.

"Aren't you tired?" she asked as he set her down.

He laughed under his breath. "You have no idea how far I can take this." *Want to take this* would have been more accurate.

She glanced down at his erection and her eyes widened. "But you just..."

"And we both will again." He backed her up until the mattress hit the back of her knees, and they both went down laughing. He mentally added the sounds of her laughter to the list of things that chipped away at his steely resolve and laced their fingers together. Pinning them a little too roughly beside her head, he nudged her legs open wider with his knees, struggling to temper the feeling of fullness in his chest. He'd dreamed of seeing her lying beneath him so many times it should be easy to keep his emotions in check, but nothing compared to reality. Seeing her gorgeous face on his pillow, her eyes turned up to him with warmth and want, feeling her soft body conforming to his muscles. He'd found nirvana, and he never wanted to leave.

He rocked his hips, pressing his cock against her wetness. "Damn." His head fell forward. "Condom."

Amanda tightened her fingers between his, her beguiling eyes wreaking havoc with him. She absently licked her lips, tearing down another barrier he'd erected.

"But you said you're clean."

"I am." He knew the minute he drove into her with nothing between them it would be that much harder to walk away. *Another broken rule. Another line crossed.*

"Then." She lifted her shoulder in a too-damn-adorable shrug.

She was offering herself to him, and if he didn't accept, would he spend the rest of his life regretting it? *Damn it. Now* he would.

"Amanda, this isn't going anywhere between us. You know that, right? I don't do relationships." *No matter how badly I want to, and right now I want you never to walk out that door again.*

"I know, but it's our one night," she said so sweetly he got goose bumps. A spark of heat flared in her eyes. "Why not make the best of it?"

"Fuck," he mumbled.

"Never mind." The excitement in her eyes dimmed, slaying him anew. "I'm asking for more than what you offered. I'm sorry. I just...You're right. It's better this way."

"You didn't ask for too much." *I did. The minute I offered to crack your conservative shell.* "I haven't had unprotected sex." His next thought pissed him off, but he said it anyway. "Just promise me you'll be careful with other guys. Seriously. I don't want anything happening to you."

A flicker of something he couldn't decipher passed through her eyes, and then she smiled like he'd just bought her diamonds. "I promise!"

"Baby, you're killing me in the best possible way."

Mick took her in a greedy kiss as he thrust into her tight, hot center. They both moaned at the immense pleasure, and when he was buried to the hilt, they both stilled.

"Mick. God, Mick. You feel so good. Too good. Oh my God. I didn't expect..."

"Shh, baby. Your voice. It drives me crazy."

"It does?" She blinked several times, a playful smile lifting her lips.

"Christ," he mumbled. "Yes, and you're so tight I want to stay buried deep inside you all night."

"It's been a long time," she said softly.

His heart squeezed with her confession. *So trusting.*

She turned her eyes to their locked hands, then back to his face. "I want to touch you."

The desire in her voice slithered beneath his skin, and his walls came crashing down. He smothered her lips with demanding mastery, and their bodies moved with the urgency of long-lost lovers. Their skin grew slick with sweat as they thrust and slid, arched and groped. Sounds of their lovemaking filled the room, moans, pleas, and the harsh sounds of flesh on flesh. The air around them sizzled in the moon's glow. Their kisses were deep and torturous. Mick reared up, angling his hips and thrusting deeper, gazing down at the beautiful woman beneath him.

"Look at me, baby," he said without a hint of

command, too caught up in the moment to care that he'd lost his distance. He'd never forget this, the way she was looking at him, like she saw only him, wanted only him.

He brought his mouth to her wrist and kissed her there, grinding his hips in slow circles, rubbing against all the sensitive places he'd discovered earlier.

"Mick, that's...That's..."

He wanted to touch her in ways she'd never been touched and craved the discovery of all of her erogenous zones. He dragged his tongue from her wrist to the tender skin at the crook of her elbow, lingering there as she began to tremble. He used his teeth, then his tongue again, and she moaned and arched. Her eyes slammed closed and she bowed off the bed. He lowered his mouth to her breast as the orgasm gripped her, and she cried out his name.

"That's it, baby. I'm going to hear that scream in my dreams." He was on the verge of coming, but he wasn't done. He wanted to—*had to*—see her riding him. In one easy move he gathered her in his arms and rolled to his back, never breaking their connection. She was like a goddess, with the moonlight at her back and her hair curtaining her gorgeous face.

She pinned his hands beside his head with a wicked gleam in her eyes. "I think I might like this."

"You've never...?"

She shook her head. The pleasure he took from racking up all these *firsts* was sinful.

"Ride me, baby."

And she did. Hard. Fast. Slow. *Maddeningly* slow. Then fast again, taking him right up to the edge. He sat up, guided her legs around his waist, and claimed her in another deep, possessive kiss.

"Your mouth," he said between kisses. "How will I ever get enough of your mouth?"

Her head fell back and her fingers dug into his biceps as she came. He sealed his mouth over her neck, sucking as her sex pulsed around his cock. He wanted to take her from behind, against the wall, in the shower, in the ass. His mind was spinning tales of what could never be. He shifted her onto her back, taking her in another rough kiss. In a futile attempt to fuck the thoughts out of his head, he pounded into her, holding her so tight not even air could fit between them. But no matter how hard he tried, he couldn't shake the feeling that what they were doing was definitely not just fucking.

"Mick. I'm gonna...again. Oh G—"

He buried his face in the crook of her neck and surrendered to his own explosive release. He came, and came, and came, until he had nothing left to give. And then he held her for a long, long time, a full-on war raging in his head. He listened to the cadence of her breathing, felt her heartbeat calm, and reveled in the feel of her going soft in his arms again.

"I should leave," she whispered. "The book says never to sta..." Her voice trailed off.

"Book?" His question fell on deaf ears. She'd already succumbed to the numbed sleep of a satiated lover.

This is when I should show you the front door. He pulled her in closer, despite knowing he shouldn't. *Get up.* He closed his eyes against his conscience. He didn't understand what was going on in his mind. He didn't do sleepovers, and he sure as hell shouldn't do one with the woman who had already mind-fucked him so badly she was in his bed. And then it dawned on him.

This was their only night, and his greedy body wanted more. This wasn't going to be over until he knew the pleasure of spooning her. A few minutes of feeling her sweet body safe and warm against him and he'd be ready to call her a cab, call it a night, and move on from the most exquisite night of his life.

He shifted positions, holding her right where he wanted her, and she nuzzled in. Their bodies fit so perfectly together it was like they were made for each other. *This* was what he needed. She sighed in her sleep, her fingers curled around his, and just for a minute, he closed his eyes.

**

AMANDA AWOKE TO the feel of something hard against her backside and a very male, very muscular body encircling her. *Ohmygod. I never left.* Her eyes darted around the room. She'd slept in Mick's bed. She'd slept *with* Mick. She'd *fucked* Mick. Her boss. Her mystery man. Her fantasy. She couldn't even blame it on being drunk. She was just stupid. Flat-out stupid. And now he was going to wake up and remember her—*sucking his dick*. She slammed her eyes shut to escape that image, and their night of debauchery came back in full detail: her pleas, her screams, his dirty promises, his mouth, his touch. *God, your mouth.* He should patent his mouth. Now she was hot and bothered again! How did he do that? He wasn't even awake! She had to get out of there. But if she moved, he'd wake up. Where were her clothes? *Downstairs. By the bar.* He'd done incredible things to her on that bar. He'd had his finger in her ass on that bar. She cringed.

This sucked.

She sucked.

Yes, I did. Well, that part didn't suck at *all.*

And swallowed.

Oh Lord.

Regret *was* the emotion du jour, and it came rushing in, thickening the air around her and making it hard to breathe. She needed to leave. To quit her job. Maybe even move away. How far could she go? Would he give her a reference? A good one? Oh no. What if she'd sucked at everything last night? He'd said sexy, complimentary things, but that was in the heat of the moment. And really what could he say? *Gee, you really suck at giving head?* How could she ever face him again?

She had to get the heck out of there. She needed a plan. She could run from the room, but that would make her look like an idiot. Not to mention that she was sore in places she never knew could get sore. She made a mental note to join a gym. Immediately. She could try to play it cool, but she wasn't cool enough to pretend to be cool. Especially after their mind-blowing sexfest and perfect kisses. Oh, how she'd loved those kisses! She shouldn't love those kisses. It was one night. *One night of pleasure. A fantasy. No strings. No regrets.* She'd done great with the first three, but she was screwed on the regret thing.

Just one night and we'll never speak of it again.

She clung to his promise. Maybe he'd wake up and they really wouldn't speak of it. They'd pretend as if they always walked around naked, the two of them in his apartment, and then she'd get dressed and leave. Monday morning they'd act like it had never happened.

That possibility made her feel a little better. He was experienced. Surely he *knew* to do that.

His arm tightened around her middle, and his cock—his beautiful, talented cock—lodged between her ass cheeks. She went damp and buried her face in the pillow. Maybe he had a gun and she could save them both the embarrassment and shoot herself.

He pressed a kiss just below her ear, and she froze.

"Freckles?" he whispered sleepily. "You're still here?" His body tensed, and he bolted upright. "Freckles. You're still here."

Okay, so maybe he wasn't as experienced as she'd hoped.

The shock in his voice made her wish for that gun again. He might as well have said, *What the fuck are you still doing here?*

"I'm leaving. I'm sorry. I must have fallen asleep." She clung to the sheet and moved to get up, but he swept her beneath him and looked at her like he was trying to figure out how they'd ended up here.

"Calm down," he said casually. How'd he tuck away his panic so fast?

She pressed her lips together in an attempt to silence her mounting panic, but it bubbled out anyway. "I can't. I'm sorry. We shouldn't have. I...How can I calm down? I have to leave. Like, right now."

She leaned up, expecting him to move, but he remained an immovable wall of stupid, sexy muscles. His piercing stare brought back every seductive look he'd given her last night, and his cocky grin made her all sorts of confused. "Don't look at me like that. I'm formally giving you my resignation. Right now. Forget last night. Please. God, please."

"Why?" he asked with an amused chuckle.

"Stop enjoying my mental breakdown. I'll tell you why. Because we did all those dirty things, and I was supposed to be learning, and all I did was let you give me orgasm after orgasm after orgasm after..." She winced. "You get the picture. And I shouldn't have stayed over."

"Because 'the book' says so."

"Ohmygod. You know about the book?" *Holy crap, what else did I say?*

He cocked a brow.

"Okay, I can explain. *The Handbook: Release Your Inner Temptress* came highly recommended, and it was helpful—" Her words were smothered by his mouth, as were her thoughts and her anxiety, until all that was left was the feeling that she was floating on a cloud.

With Mick.

No, no, no!

Yes, yes, yes!

She pushed at his chest, and he groaned as he pried his mouth from her.

"Did *The Handbook* advise you to push a guy away when he kisses you? If so, that book has to go."

"Mick! We said one night and we'd never speak of it again. I ruined everything. I didn't even *try* to seduce you beyond the whole, well, you know, what we did on the steps. You didn't get to critique my seduction skills, and now I'm left comparing every man out there to you, which believe me, will suck for me *and* them. Not to mention that I'm in no better shape than I was before last night. I still have no idea if I'm doing things right, and I'm sore in places I never knew could get sore." She realized she was rambling and clamped her big mouth shut.

His brows knitted. "You're right."

"I know." She didn't know what she'd been hoping for, but disappointment skated in, and she smacked the mattress. "I'm sorry. I suck."

"I do like the way you suck." His wicked grin was back.

She loved that wicked grin.

Ugh! He was totally messing with her! She swatted his arm. "Stop it. No more talking about what we did. Now get up."

"No."

"No?"

"No. I can't let you go out in the world doing what some stupid book advises. That would be irresponsible of me. You need to be properly schooled in all things seductive. What choice do we have but to spend the weekend together?"

"Mick." *Weekend? Is he nuts?* He seemed as shocked by his idea as she was. Or maybe that was cockiness; she couldn't be sure.

"I'm serious. I have a reputation to uphold. If you go out and tell even one person that I didn't live up to my promise, all hell might break loose."

"I'm *never* speaking of this. Not even to Ally." *Oh God, Ally!* She'd probably texted a hundred times to make sure Amanda was still alive. Mick looked at her sideways, and she knew he was wondering if she could really keep something like this from her sister. He knew how close they were, and Ally was living with, and engaged to, his childhood friend Heath Wild.

"Obviously we won't speak of our Adventure Sex Weekend," he said casually. "That would also be irresponsible."

"Wait, what? Adventure Sex Weekend?"

"It's the only way. We've already crossed a line we can't uncross." His tone turned serious. "Let's do this right. You'll spend the whole weekend seducing me, of course."

He was right about crossing the line. *Holy cow. Am I really considering this?*

"You sound like you're talking about a client meeting."

"It's an arrangement of sorts," he said. "An agreement. A weekend of seduction, no regrets afterward, and for God's sake, no resignations, either."

"Mick, how am I going to look at you in the office?"

He brushed a lock of hair from her shoulder and pressed a kiss there. "The same way you always have." He held her gaze, steady, dark. *Seductive.* "You want this, Amanda. One weekend. No strings. And no one has to know."

She felt herself not only considering a weekend with Mick, but giving in to the quickening of her pulse and the ache between her legs. All her best parts were pulling for Mick's plan, but her conservative, careful side thought this was a bad idea.

He pressed a kiss to the corner of her mouth, sending ripples of anticipation through her. *I'm already in too deep.*

"I think we should start right now," he whispered. "Come on, freckles. You want this."

God help her, she did. So very badly.

He rolled onto his back and linked his hands behind his head. The sheets bunched beside him, every hard muscle and his perfect, eager penis on display. How could she deny herself this pleasure? She'd have to be blind and deaf, and even that wouldn't be enough, because she knew how he felt, how he tasted.

He ran his finger along her jaw. "You want this, baby."

Baby.

She'd have to wipe her senses clean. Erase every memory.

Right after the weekend.

Chapter Six

"IT'S ME. I'M sorry I didn't answer your calls, but I'm fine." Amanda pulled her cell phone away from her ear as Ally reamed her out for not responding to her messages last night. She had twenty minutes before Mick was picking her up. She still couldn't believe she'd agreed to a weekend of sex and seduction. Who did she think she was? Marilyn Monroe?

"Seriously. I was up all night, and if it weren't for Heath, I'd have called the cops. You owe him big-time." Ally huffed out a frustrated breath. "I swear, Mandy, when I see you, I'm going to kick your ass."

"I know," she said, glancing in the mirror as Ally told her *again* how irresponsible she'd been. But it had been worth it. She'd had the most amazing, if not confusing, night. And this morning had been equally incredible. After she and Mick had devoured each other, she'd come home to shower and pack. It was September, and it was supposed to be a breezy seventy degrees this weekend. With that *and* seduction in mind, she'd spent forever choosing today's outfit: a pair of high-heeled, fringed beige boots, a short brown skirt, and a white button-down blouse, unbuttoned all the way down to her front-clasping bra, which she was still feeling uncomfortable about—the cleavage, not the bra.

"I'm sorry, Al. I *really* am. But I need your help." Mick was used to being seduced by rich, beautiful women. She hoped she wouldn't disappoint him, and more importantly, the following thoughts had become her new mantra. *This isn't real. It's a weekend arrangement. A business agreement. Nothing more.*

"Oh God. See?" Ally said. "You're not fine. What happened? Who were you with? I'll come over right now."

She pictured her sister gathering her purse and keys. "No! Don't come over. I'm leaving soon, and I can't tell you who I was with anyway. But you know him, and I'm safe with him."

"Amanda, what is going on? Where do I know him from?"

Amanda pulled open her underwear drawer, trying to ignore the demand in Ally's voice. Remembering Mick's affinity for black lace, she sifted through her cotton panties for her new black lace thongs and matching bras and tossed them on the bed.

"I'm spending the weekend—" *Seducing my boss.* She froze. *This is not smart.*

"With...?" Ally prompted, pulling Amanda from her thoughts.

Just this once she didn't want to be the smart, careful sister. "With the guy from the bar crawl."

"Mandy, this is *not* okay. Tell me who he is."

"I can't. But I do need your help. What would you

wear for a weekend where your sole purpose is seducing a man? I know I need a sexy dress or two. Do you think I can wear jeans, too? Or is that too—"

"Amanda! If you don't spill your guts right this second, I swear I'll handcuff you to something in my apartment and you won't be able to leave."

Handcuffs. Hm. She wondered if Mick was into that. *Am I? Could I be?* She wanted to tell Ally what she'd done. Ally always told her everything— *everything except what I needed to know about this particular subject.* No, Amanda decided. She wasn't going to break the promise of secrecy she'd made to Mick.

"It's not a huge deal." It was bigger than huge, but she didn't need to admit that to her already worried sister. "I just agreed to spend the weekend with him." She picked out two cute dresses and tossed them on the bed.

"You said I know him. From where?"

"You just do. I'm not telling you, so..."

"Amanda, do I have to worry? Or are you really okay? He's already asked you to spend the weekend together, so obviously you don't need my advice on seducing him." Ally gasped. "Oh no. He's not married is he? Because you can't put yourself in that position."

"No! He's not married. It's complicated. He's a business associate. I'm really okay, Al. You don't have to worry. I promise." That last little fib left a sour taste in her mouth. Amanda wasn't okay. She was worried. Not for her safety, but for her heart. She had no idea how she'd face Mick at work and act like nothing had happened between them. She'd only been half kidding about resigning, but that was true regardless of whether they spent this weekend together or not.

They'd already blown way past all the lines that would make remaining at the firm easy *or* appropriate, despite his demand of *no resignations.*

"Ally?" Amanda moved quickly, aware she had only a few minutes left to pack and pull herself together. She chose a casual outfit, shoes, nighties— *nighties?* The man was a sex machine. She doubted she'd get much wear out of any of her clothes.

"I'm here."

Amanda gathered her toiletries and stuffed them into a bag. "I'm not trying to shut you out. It really is complicated. Meet me Monday night at the Kiss?"

Ally sighed. "I didn't know you still went there."

The Kiss was an artsy bar in the Village. Every Monday night they held romance readings where aspiring writers read romantic passages they'd written. Amanda and Ally had stumbled upon it together before Ally met Heath, and Amanda continued to go every Monday night.

A knock on her door sent her heart racing. "He's here. I have to go. Meet me there? At the Kiss? At seven?"

"Okay. Be safe. I'm going to text you tonight and tomorrow, and if you don't respond by midnight, I *will* call the police."

"Okay! Love you." She ended the call and zipped up her bags, wondering if she was taking too much and if she'd chosen the right clothes. Spotting her perfume on the dresser, she shoved that into her bag. Another knock brought self-doubt. She hurried out of her bedroom and stopped at the front door.

I can't do this.

Yes, you can.

Her eyes darted around her tiny apartment. She'd

loved the cozy space from the moment she'd walked in the first time, despite its size. And Mick, who owned a *three-story* apartment, was about to see it. Maybe she should tell him she was sick.

Her cell phone vibrated on the table by the door. She grabbed it, prepared to tell Ally she was really fine, despite World War Mick raging in her head. The sight of Mick's name on the screen made her stomach flutter. She opened and read the text.

Seduction rule #1. You must be in the same room with the person you're trying to seduce.

She smiled and looked out the peephole in the door, but he was looking down and all she saw was his dark hair. A second later her phone vibrated with another text.

You want this, Amanda. Open the door.

She did. She wanted this. She wanted *him*, any way she could have him.

Without giving herself a chance to second-guess her decision, she opened the door, sighing way too dreamily at the sight of him in low-slung jeans. A pair of mirrored sunglasses hung from the collar of his gray T-shirt, which hugged his chest and shoulders, the fabric visibly straining over his biceps. He hadn't shaved, and his hair was finger combed, sexy and tousled. She was so used to seeing him in expensive suits, he looked like a different man altogether. Dangerous. Edgy. *Sinful.*

His eyes raked over her ever so slowly, as if he didn't want to miss a thing, making her feel vulnerable and excited all at once. They dropped from her breasts to her thighs, lingering there so long she shivered with the memory of his face buried between them last night. How was she going to make it through a weekend of seducing the man who made it hard for her to remember her name?

**

"HEY THERE, GORGEOUS." Mick stepped forward and kissed Amanda's cheek, because if he went for her lips, he wasn't going to stop there. She looked like a sex kitten in her short, tight skirt with her wide-eyed innocence in full play. He had no idea how he was going to hold his shit together for the next few hours, much less all weekend.

"Hi." She tugged on the hem of her skirt, staring at him like she had last night, with wonder and heat.

He waited for her to say more, knowing he needed to relinquish control and allow her room to seduce, given their agreement, but suppressing his urge to take control was killing him. Especially since she seemed to be as lost in him at the moment as he was in her. And damn, he liked that a whole hell of a lot.

He slid a hand along her waist and whispered, "You should probably invite me in so we can get your stuff."

"Oh! Right, sorry. Come in." She stepped aside and closed the door behind him.

Mick took in the classic yet elegant feel of her cozy apartment, which suited Amanda perfectly. A white sofa and love seat created a nook by the windows, backing to pale blue walls trimmed in white. On the far wall, two white bookshelves held a myriad of legal books, romance novels, and other literary works, interspersed with photographs of Amanda and her family. He briefly wondered if she'd told Ally about last night or this weekend.

Amanda pointed down the hallway to his right. "I'll get my bags."

Keeping hold of her waist, he said, "Seduction, remember?"

Her brow wrinkled in confusion.

"Men like to feel needed."

"Oh. Um..."

"You might ask me to carry your bags because they're too heavy."

"But they're not that—" Her mouth gaped, and an adorable blush bloomed on her cheeks. She stepped closer, her eyes widening with feigned innocence. "Um, Mick?" She ran her finger down the center of his chest, sending heat further south. "Would you mind helping me with my bags? They're a little heavy." She licked her lips, and just like that, he got hard, remembering her lips wrapped around his cock last night. "They're in the *bedroom*."

"Christ," he muttered. "We may never leave your apartment."

"Oh no. I'm that bad?"

He tightened his hold on her and rocked his arousal against her so she could feel the effect she had on him. "No, baby. You're that good."

This weekend was a dangerous idea, but last night hadn't been enough. Spooning her hadn't been enough. Waking up with her in his arms hadn't been enough. This weekend *had* to be enough. She'd learn what she needed to meet the type of men she wanted—a thought that twisted him into knots—he'd convince her she didn't need to resign, and come Monday, they'd have had their fill of each other and be capable of moving on.

Yeah, and pigs fly.

What other choice did he have? He wasn't about to throw himself into a relationship, which is exactly what she deserved, only not with a guy like him. He was too cynical. He would spend every day waiting for the shoe to drop. This was the only way. Get his fill, get her out of his system, and go back to the way things were.

With that in mind, he told himself not to linger in her bedroom, but the minute he stepped beyond the threshold, he was sucked into her world. White sheers hung from an iron canopy above the bed. Pale pink curtains framed two windows. Between them was a dressing table, the old-fashioned kind he'd seen in movies, draped in lace, with a vase of fresh flowers sitting on top. Another bouquet of flowers sat atop a dresser by the closet. The room smelled like a meadow after a light rain. On the bedside table were candles and more romance novels. He reluctantly glanced at the burnt wicks and couldn't help but wonder what lucky bastard had been in her bed. His gut fisted with the thought. This was a side of her she might never have revealed. Although he knew she was a sucker for romance, he never imagined it went this deep. Her bedroom conflicted sharply with the skills she was trying to hone, and he fought the urge to tell her she didn't need to do this. Not with him, or for any man. But that wasn't his place. He'd already put himself in enough of a conundrum.

Picking up her bag, he turned and found her fidgeting with her skirt again and was struck anew by the conflicting messages. He had no idea why knowing she was a romantic at heart bothered him so much, but it did. The thought of some unworthy man—or men—touching her had always bothered him, but now it made his blood boil. What on earth had made him think he would be okay with teaching Amanda how to seduce other men?

"You like romance," he said sharply. He was pissed at himself, because while he had the means and the desire to give her anything and everything she wanted, he was a prisoner of his past and of his mind—too smart to believe in the happily-ever-after fantasy she craved.

She smiled. "Don't all women?"

"Maybe." *But I don't give a shit about them.* "But they don't all deserve to find it."

A few minutes later they were heading out of the city in his Aston Martin One-77. Amanda looked out the window. Her hair had caught on her shoulder, giving him a glimpse of the freckles below her ear. He wanted to lean over and kiss them. He wondered about his fascination with her freckles, chalking it up to being no different from knowing the way she liked her coffee, or that she licked her lips when she was nervous. They were intimate glimpses into the woman he'd been falling for—and trying not to. If he were honest with himself, he'd admit that his mind had become a web, collecting pieces of Amanda he never wanted to forget. But that kind of honesty took introspection, and introspection brought back the past.

No, thank you.

"Tell me about *The Handbook*," he said to distract himself as he pulled onto the highway. "I need to know what I have to help you unlearn."

"It's too embarrassing," she said, still looking out the window.

"Even after last night?" He reached for her hand in

an effort to ease her nerves—and to soothe his need to be closer to her.

She turned, the determined set of her jaw a smoke screen for the uncertainty in her eyes. She wasn't cut out for the world of one-night stands and meaningless seductions. He added another item to her weekend lessons—convincing her that learning to seduce was one thing, but she didn't need to take it further than making a future date. One-night stands were off-limits.

"Baby." As soon as the endearment slipped out, he knew he had to rein it back in. He didn't use endearments with women. Then again, he didn't take women to his apartment—or his home in Sweetwater, New York, where they were headed now.

"It's a book," he reassured her. "We can talk about a book. Wanting to explore your sensuality shouldn't be embarrassing, and certainly not with me."

"You're my *boss*," she said quietly. Then stronger, "Of course it should be embarrassing. Maybe we're making a mistake."

He should take that opportunity to turn the car around and escape the tangled web they were weaving. He should solidify the walls he'd lived behind for so long. He knew this, and he fought against it, because if he did, he'd spend the rest of his life wondering what this weekend could have been like.

"We can turn around," he offered, "but it won't erase what we did last night. And come Monday that's still going to be there. We won't talk about it, and we'll try to act like it didn't happen. But last night will *always* be there. Our secret. What happens between now and Monday isn't going to change the outcome Monday will bring."

She looked out the window again, stealing her

hand from his.

"If you're worried about respect, or that I'll see you differently, you're right."

She shot him a pained expression.

"I respect you *more* for wanting to explore all sides of yourself and for being brave enough to do it. I've gotten to know more about you in the last twenty-four hours than I have in the last three years."

She continued staring at him as he drove. He felt her silently assessing him, and he wondered what she saw. He wondered what he'd see if he looked in a mirror, and made a point of not doing it.

"You're really hard to read right now."

"Am I?" He glanced at her and smiled.

"I can't tell if you mean it, like you really do respect me more, or if you're placating me so I don't feel cheap for sleeping with you."

That wiped his smile away, and he shook his head. "Then don't sleep with me. This seduction weekend is for you. You control what we do, how far we go. I'm just along to critique and make sure you know enough to keep yourself from getting into trouble." *And to satiate myself enough to be able to walk away without losing my mind.*

She laughed. "I'm supposed to believe you're that altruistic? Please, Mick. Don't act like I'm a fool. You're in it for the sex."

"Am I?" He was, partially, but not just for sex. For sex *with Amanda. Time* with Amanda. He didn't fully understand all the reasons he'd suggested this weekend, but he knew *not* being with her wasn't an option. He needed to get her out of his system once and for all.

He glanced at her again. There was no fooling her.

She was as brilliant as she was sweet, and the combination, he decided, was the biggest aphrodisiac there was. No, he took that back. Brilliance and sweetness all wrapped up in Amanda Jenner was the biggest aphrodisiac.

"If that were true," he said with another smile, "we wouldn't have left your bedroom."

"I guess you have a point." She rested her head back and closed her eyes. "Where are we going anyway? Aren't we staying at your place?"

"We are," he assured her. "Just not my place in the city."

She sat up straight. "You have another house?"

"You agreed to spend the weekend with a man without doing your research? What kind of paralegal are you?" That earned him an eye roll *and* a smile— and boy did he like her smile. "You'll like it. I promise. Now, let's talk about that book."

Chapter Seven

AMANDA CAVED AND told Mick about *The Handbook*, what she'd learned and how it had helped her gain the confidence to come out of her shell a little more each week. They'd talked for more than an hour. He listened intently, nodding and tossing out a comment here and there. She was glad he hadn't reamed her about how stupid she was for trying to learn from a book, but she wondered what he really thought about it—and about her. Some of the looks he was giving her made her stomach flip and dip, and then his expression would turn serious again, reminding her of the confines of their agreement.

He turned off the highway. "Thank you for sharing all of that with me," he said with a thoughtful smile. A few minutes later they turned onto a narrow road bordered by lush forests bursting with rich reds, vibrant yellows, greens, browns, and every color in between. They rolled down the windows, and she inhaled the scents of autumn as they followed the winding road up a mountain.

"Where are we?"

"The Silver Mountains. I thought you'd be more comfortable somewhere where you wouldn't worry about running into people you knew. That way there's no need for a wig."

Or is it because you don't want anyone you know to see us together? The thought lingered like an itch she couldn't scratch, despite the fact that if he was telling her the truth, it was quite a thoughtful gesture. *And a reminder that you probably have a lot of experience with meaningless sexual encounters to have thought of such a thing.*

"That was smart," she said. "Then neither of us has to worry. It would be embarrassing to see someone we work with."

He was quiet for a minute, the muscle in his jaw jumping like a pulse.

"Right," he said tightly. "We're heading to Sweetwater, a small town Heath's brother Logan turned me on to a few years back. He's got a cabin here."

She wondered if he'd told Logan about their weekend. Cringing inwardly, she wondered if Logan told Heath, who would tell Ally—who would kill her for not only not telling her, but also for having sex with her boss. She chewed on that uncomfortable thought, her stomach twisting and turning tighter by the second, until she remembered that Mick had been just as adamant about never speaking of their time together as she was.

"Do you?" she asked. "Have a cabin, I mean?"

"No, no cabin."

He had no cabin? Were they staying at Logan's

after all? She debated texting Ally and telling her the truth, but what if Mick hadn't told Logan? Her heart was beating so hard she felt like she might explode.

"Did you tell Logan about last night? About this weekend?"

His face contorted like he'd eaten something that tasted bad. "I thought you trusted me."

"I do, but we're going somewhere you don't have a cabin and he does, so I thought..."

He shook his head and said coldly, "Number one, I try not to lie—"

"I know, but I didn't tell Ally, and I don't want her to find out from Heath, who might find out from Logan. I hate deceiving her."

His expression softened. "Amanda, if you'll feel better telling your sister, then by all means please do. I trust your judgment, but you should know that I haven't said anything to Logan or anyone else. When we stopped for gas and you were in the restroom, Brett called. I told him I was heading to Sweetwater for the weekend, but he knows I don't—" He winced. "He'd have no reason to think I was with you."

"Okay, thanks." Brett was Mick's youngest brother. He and their brother Carson, an IT expert, owned an international security company. Amanda liked all three of Mick's younger brothers, having met them at various times in the office and at NightCaps, a bar Mick's brother Dylan owned.

"Really, baby, if you want to tell your sister, please do. I don't want you to worry."

"It's okay. I just didn't want her to find out from someone else."

He stared out at the road. "You grew up outside of the city, didn't you? Was it like this?"

She was surprised he remembered. They hadn't talked about where she was from since she'd first come to the firm. "It was rural, but not in the mountains like this. This is prettier than a postcard. I love the fall. It makes me think of evening walks with leaves swirling around my feet, all wrapped up in a thick cozy sweater."

"If you're trying to seduce a man, you might want to forget the sweater and mention something about *him* keeping you warm."

His suggestion didn't embarrass her. Talking about the book, and her preparatory weeks leading up to the bar crawl, had brought them to a different place. Bound them together with another secret. Although, that deeper connection stirred other feelings. Her heart still held on to the hope that this weekend might lead to something more, and she had a feeling that internal battle was going to be her constant companion until Monday. There wasn't much she could do but try to accept it.

If she was going to do this, she was definitely going to do it right. "See? That's exactly why I need you. To remind me of those little things that make a world of difference." She dug her *Handbook* out of her purse and scribbled that down.

"You're taking notes?"

"Of course. A very wise man once told me to always take notes, even if I think I might not need them, because I—"

"Might decipher them differently later," they said in unison.

She laughed and stuffed the book back in her bag. She made a mental note to remember she was supposed to be in full-on seduction mode from here on out and to be on the lookout for chances to test her knowledge.

"I think living in the city takes away from the beauty of the seasons, don't you? I'd forgotten how inspiring autumn feels." She turned and caught him watching her. "What? Did I miss a chance to be seductive?"

"No." He laughed. "You looked happy just then. Happy looks good on you."

"I'm pretty happy all the time, aren't I?" Wasn't she? She felt like she was.

"In the three years we've known each other, I've only seen you angry a handful of times and sad *three* times. Otherwise, yeah. I think you're usually in a good mood."

"Thank you, but when have you seen me sad? I try to keep my emotions out of the office." *Other than lust, which seems to follow me like a shadow when I'm around you.*

He tightened his grip on the steering wheel.

"Mick? You can't tell me you've seen me sad *three* times and then pretend you don't know when those times were. Three is a very specific number."

"Maybe I'm wrong."

"You're never wrong."

He grinned at that.

"Spill it." She crossed her arms and glared at him, wondering if he'd made it up after all.

"About a month after you started, you came to work teary-eyed because you'd seen a bird fly into a window."

She remembered that morning. The poor thing had flown into a window and plopped to the ground. No one had stopped to see if it was okay but her. Mick had stopped by her office to give her a file and parked himself beside her, resting his butt against her desk, and refused to leave until she told him why she was upset. *Probably a broken neck*, he'd said, and then he'd hugged her. She'd never forgotten how tender he was, and she'd never seen him hug another employee in all the time they'd worked together.

"And then when that guy cheated on Ally," he said with a pitch of annoyance. "You were so mad, you wanted to kill him. But the next day, all that anger had turned to sadness because your sister was so upset."

She was surprised, and touched, that he remembered these instances so clearly. "You asked if I wanted you to take out a hit on the guy."

"I wanted to kill the asshole." He clenched his jaw. "I hated seeing you unhappy."

She soaked his confession in, unsure of what to make of it.

"The third time," he said with a heavy tone, "was Thursday night, when I realized it was you and stopped before we...had a chance to finish."

She turned away, remembering her confusion at his abrupt halt. "I was hurt, not sad."

"Aren't they the same thing?" He reached over, gently taking her chin in his hand, and turned her toward him. His eyes moved between her and the road. "I'm sorry. I never meant to hurt you, but I couldn't do that with you there."

Her heart skipped at the sincerity in his voice and the tenderness of his gaze.

"You deserve far more than a quick fuck in the bathroom of a bar, and don't ever let anyone make you think otherwise. We'll put that into your lesson plan— taking control of *where* and *when*."

Her skipping heart stopped cold. She really needed to stop reading into the things he said, or she was never going to make it through the weekend.

"But if I were anyone else, you probably would have gone through with it," she said sharply. "So are you saying *you're* not worth more than that?"

He was silent for so long she didn't think he was going to respond. "That's a good question."

Amanda reminded herself again not to read too much into the things he said—or the things he didn't.

**

MICK COULDN'T STOP thinking about Amanda's question. Was he worth more than a quick fuck in the bathroom of a bar? Hell yes, in all the ways that counted. He was at the top of his field, and he hadn't gotten there by lying, cheating, or scamming. His father had unknowingly taught him well in that regard. Gerard Bad was a bastard of an attorney, as manipulative and devious as they came, and he was also one of the leading criminal law attorneys in the city. Criminal law was very different from entertainment law, and to some extent his father had to play the game, but Mick didn't care. After his sister had passed away, his father had turned darker, meaner, and hateful toward his family and the rest of the world. Mick looked like his father, and in his younger years, everyone who knew them commented about how he was a *chip off the old block*. Mick had vowed never to be that chip. His decision to go into law was based on his need to deal with facts and truths. Right and wrong was definable, unlike so many other things. Driven by the need to prove to his father there was a better way to handle things, he worked hard to make his mark without using the tactics his father relied on, and it served him well.

But that didn't mean Mick was worth more than a quick fuck in the bathroom of a bar, because his father had also taught him that love wasn't real. And losing Lorelei had taught Mick that nothing lasted forever. A lethal combination for any relationship, one that dealing in cold, hard facts had reinforced many times over. He'd long ago sworn off having a family of his own. The thought of losing a child—and in turn, the people he loved, as his father had—was overwhelming. He might have dodged the DNA bullet in the asshole-attorney department, but no man dodged two bullets in one lifetime.

"Mick!" Amanda gasped as Sugar Lake came into view, pulling Mick from his thoughts. "This is gorgeous."

She *ooh*ed and *aah*ed over the quaint little town. Mick focused on her excitement, pushing his own ugly thoughts aside. It was easier to let things go in Sweetwater, where mornings were defined by the sun rising over the mountains and what time Willow Dalton opened her bakery. Afternoons were marked by children's voices as they ran home from school, and evenings lasted as long as neighbors were willing to chat on the porch, or at the local pub. Logan had given Mick the gift of a lifetime when he'd introduced him to the small town. This was where he came when he felt the tug for a future he'd never have.

"Welcome to Sweetwater," he said. He might not be able to give Amanda the romantic love she wanted and deserved, but he could give her this weekend, which was more than he'd ever given any other woman.

"Look!" She pointed to a banner hanging above the cobblestone street just down the road that read, SWEETWATER FALL FESTIVAL.

"I forgot this was the weekend of the festival." He parked by the lake, across the street from his house. He had a garage out back, but he loved seeing Amanda so excited and didn't want to cheat her out of enjoying the views. A grassy lawn led to the sandy shore of the lake, which was larger than Lake George and twice as beautiful. Set against the backdrop of the Silver Mountains, with the bustling fairgrounds in the distance to their left, the glassy lake stretched to the horizon. Behind them, rows of old-fashioned shops with big picture windows and large awnings lined the cobblestone streets.

Amanda threw open her door and stepped out before Mick had a chance to walk around and open it for her.

She inhaled deeply. "This is gorgeous! And not that far from the city."

She set her hands on her hips and glared at him, a look he'd seen a million times in the office when he'd asked her to complete a near-impossible task. Only now she wore a short, tight skirt that accentuated her slim waist and full hips, and her breasts were seriously straining the buttons on her blouse, making it hard for him to think of anything other than the sweet slice of heaven standing before him.

"Mick Bad," she said with a wide smile and a serious tone. "What other secrets are you keeping from me?"

If you only knew.

"What kind of way is that to talk to a man you're

trying to seduce?" he teased. "I thought you studied *The Handbook*."

Her eyes instantly went from glaring to apologetic, making him wish he hadn't said it.

"You're right. I forgot. It's hard to be that way all the time. Do I really have to? I mean, is that the best way for me to learn?" She leaned into the car to grab her purse, giving him an enticing view of her perfect ass.

"I really do suck at this." She plunked her purse on the seat and began rifling through it.

He couldn't resist taking hold of her hips. He loved her hips. She wasn't rail thin like most of the women he came into contact with. She was curvy and real, and he hated that she wanted to learn to play the games most women relied on. She didn't need those things. But she wasn't here for *him*. She was here to *use* him. To *practice*. He reluctantly swallowed that jagged pill.

She straightened, holding *The Handbook*—the one he wanted to burn—against her chest and turned in his arms.

"I'm ready," she said breathlessly.

That was all it took for him to get lost in her sweet smile and trusting eyes. She must have mistaken his silence for expectation of a performance, because her entire face turned intense and focused, like when she researched a case. Her tongue swept across her lower lip, leaving it slick and enticing, and leaving him itching for a taste. She pressed her hand to his chest and opened her mouth as if to speak, but no words came.

Her brow wrinkled, and she whispered, "I'm not sure what to say," with a sexy smile.

He didn't stand a chance against that smile, those

eyes, her voice.

"Baby, that's all it takes." He leaned forward and kissed her square on the lips. She fisted her hand in his shirt, snagging skin along with it, and he tugged her in tighter, deepening the kiss. And the next breath brought the moment he loved, when her resistance slipped away and her other hand came around his neck. She gave herself over to the kiss, returning his efforts fervently. The sharp corners of her book poked into his chest, suspended by the press of their bodies. Her tongue swept hungrily over his, her body melted against him, and sexy sounds of pleasure slipped from her mouth. His emotions swelled and stretched, winding around them, binding them together like cable, strong and lasting.

"Well, isn't this a sight for sore eyes?"

Amanda jumped from his arms, her cheeks red as the autumn trees. Her book plunked to the cobblestone. She nervously grabbed at her shirt, futilely trying to pull it closed across her breasts while simultaneously tugging at the hem of her skirt. It took a moment for enough blood to make its way to Mick's brain for him to function. Amanda reached for her book, and he touched her arm.

"I've got it," he reassured her, then turned to greet his friend Willow as he retrieved it. Logan introduced Mick to Willow and her family when he'd first come house hunting in Sweetwater, and they'd become as close as family.

"Nice to see you, Willow." He handed the book to Amanda, and she clutched it to her chest. "Amanda Jenner, meet my friend Willow Dalton. Willow, this is Amanda."

"A-man-da Hug-and-kiss?" Willow teased. "Well,

you sure found a hell of a man to kiss." She pushed her long blond hair over her shoulders and pulled Amanda into an unexpected hug.

Willow was as loud and boisterous, with little interest in filtering her thoughts, as Amanda was careful and meticulous, acutely aware of every word that came out of her mouth. Although Amanda had slipped a few times over the last twenty-four hours, and Mick had found those charming, unguarded moments alarmingly appealing.

"Hi." Amanda's feet shifted nervously. "It's not like that. We're not...I'm not..."

"Oh, honey, please." Willow waved a dismissive hand. "Do *not* act like you don't want to kiss this Bad boy. Half the town wants to kiss him." She threw her arms around Mick's neck and whispered, "Piper's got your boat all ready, but I can't believe I had to hear you have a girlfriend from my sister!" Piper was one of Willow's sisters. She took care of Mick's house and boat when he was out of town. He'd called her when they'd stopped at the gas station and had asked her to set the timer for the evening lights and stock the boat with a few necessities.

Mick laughed to cover the frustration his next words would bring. "We're not a couple. We're..." *What? Fuck buddies?* Swallowing the bile rising in his throat, he said, "Working on a research project together."

"I can see that." Willow nodded to the book Amanda was holding. The title, *The Handbook: Release Your Inner Temptress,* was facing out for all to see.

"Ohmygod." Amanda threw the book in the car and closed the door. "This is so embarrassing."

Mick slid an arm around her waist. "We were only

kissing."

She turned in to him, touched her forehead to his chest, and said, "Can she still see me?"

They all laughed, but Mick's heart went warm and squishy again. He didn't usually go for cute, but he was drawn to all things *Amanda* and couldn't resist tipping her chin up and kissing her again. Her smile told him she could deal with the embarrassment just fine, and her grip on him revealed how much she liked that extra little kiss.

She turned and faced Willow, rolled her shoulders back, and held out a hand in greeting. Willow took it, with a smile so warm Mick wanted to thank her.

"Hi. I'm Amanda Jenner," she said in her *work* voice. "I'm a paralegal, and I *do* work with Mick. He's helping me with a research project. *I'm* the project, and turning up my sexy is the goal. Now it's out in the open and I can go crawl under a rock with dignity."

"Damn, girl." Willow slid her fingers into the pockets of her jeans and looked at Mick, then back at Amanda. "All you had to do was buy a book and ask him to help? You need to go on *The View*, or *Good Morning America*, because that is skill and brilliance in and of itself."

"Come Monday I'm sure I'll think it was sheer stupidity, but he's a good research partner." Amanda glanced at Mick, and he waggled his brows.

"Well, you have oodles of time between now and Monday. Are you going to join us for the Fall Festival?" Willow pointed to the fairgrounds in the distance.

"We are, if Amanda would like to," Mick answered.

"Great! Maybe I'll see you there." Willow hugged them each again and whispered, "I like her!" to Mick, before heading off toward the festival.

"I'm sorry," Amanda said as soon as Willow was out of earshot. "I didn't mean to embarrass you in front of your friend."

He could push the game further, guide her from her embarrassment and back into their lesson in seduction, but he found everything she did seductive. He was having a hell of a time holding back from acting like the man he wanted to be for Amanda.

Decision made, he let their game fall away and stepped closer, focusing on the quickening of her breaths, and as his thighs pressed to hers, the heat smoldered between them.

"New rules," he said confidently. "At night you'll be the seductress. Tonight we'll go to the pub separately, and for all intents and purposes, we'll be strangers. You'll work your magic, I'll critique, and you'll do it until you've got it down pat. It'll be your job to get me into the bedroom, but once we're there, you're *mine*."

She swallowed hard.

"Tomorrow we'll find another way for you to practice, and by the time we part Sunday night, you'll be a pro, I promise. But during the day, and in the bedroom, you're Amanda Jenner, *woman*. Not a temptress in training. Got it?"

"But...?" She slipped her finger into the waist of his jeans.

He stifled a groan. "*That* was seductive, Amanda. One finger, your innocent eyes, your breasts brushing against my chest, and I'm ready to combust. You don't need help in that area." He pressed a hand flat against her lower back, holding her against his throbbing cock.

"Oh!" Her face lit up with surprise. "Really?"

"With you? Yes." It was crazy, even to him. No

other woman had ever roused the immediate inferno Amanda did without even trying. He pushed a hand beneath her hair to the nape of her neck and brushed his thumb over her freckles. She sighed with pleasure, her long lashes fluttering with each stroke of his thumb.

"I'm attracted to you, Amanda. We have this weekend. It's all we'll ever have. I'm not cut out for relationships, and I never will be. If you want this, if you want me, you need to understand and accept that up front." He paused, letting his words settle in for both of them. Confusion and heat took up residence in her expression again.

He had to be sure they had an understanding, for both their sakes. "You can't hold on to any romantic notions that I'll change, or that I want to change, because at thirty-four, it's not going to happen. But I want this weekend, and I want you."

She breathed harder, her finger curled tightly around the waist of his jeans.

"Can you live with that? Let me be the man I want to be for you now, here, for these few days, and go back to being colleagues and friends when we return to the city? If you can't, if it makes you at all uncomfortable, we'll stick to our original plan. But I'd really like to give you, to give *us*, a weekend we'll never forget."

Chapter Eight

"I THINK I can do that." It was a fib. There was no way Amanda would be able to go back to work Monday and pretend they hadn't been together. She couldn't look at him without her heart doing a silly little happy dance. She had to continually remind herself he wasn't falling for her; he was teaching her. But now he didn't want to *teach* her? He *wanted* her? For the weekend? Wasn't this so much better than what she'd already agreed to? More confusing, certainly, because why the heck didn't he *do* relationships? But did that matter?

He wanted her, and she definitely wanted him. Their weekend promised to be even better. She'd have to come to grips with finding a new job, because turning down the most incredible offer she could ever dream of from the only man she wanted wasn't even a possibility—and his confession would make working in the same office and pretending nothing happened even more impossible.

"You're sure?" he asked. "Because I'm not playing

games this time, Amanda. When I say this is all we will ever have, and we'll leave it behind when we return to the city, I mean it."

I've got my big-girl panties on. I can handle it.

Actually, I don't have any panties on, but I can still handle it.

I hope.

She nodded curtly. "Positive, Counselor."

"I do like hearing that coming from your pretty little mouth." His lips brushed over hers. "Almost as much as I liked coming in it last night."

A tornado of heat spun inside her. His eyes dropped to her mouth. *Kiss me.* Then lower, to her shoulders, her breasts. Goose bumps rose on her flesh, her body pulsing with anticipation for whatever he'd give—a kiss, a touch, a word? Everything he did caused heart-pounding reactions.

"Would you like to change before we go to the festival, or do I get to eye-fuck you all afternoon, thinking about how easy it would be to lift that sexy little skirt and slip inside you?" He paused, and she tried to remember how to speak, which didn't seem to be happening anytime soon. He pressed his prickly scruff to her cheek, and his hot breath ghosted over her skin. "Or we can go inside and I'll fuck you now. And later."

"That." She couldn't believe she'd said it, and apparently he couldn't either, because her strong, confident, weekend-sex god blinked several times before taking her hand and dragging her across the street.

"Where are we going?" she asked, stumbling to keep up as he pulled her down a narrow alley between a café and a bookstore.

"My place. Upstairs."

"You live above the bookstore?"

"I own it." He stopped at the bottom of an iron stairway and crashed his mouth over hers, kissing her like he'd been waiting his whole life to do it.

The kiss was fast and urgent, and continued as they made their way up the stairs. He unlocked the heavy wooden door, and the second she stepped inside, he backed her up against it. The weight of their bodies slammed it closed. He grabbed her hands and pinned them above her head. His eyes went coal black, holding her captive with the promises they held. Trapping both of her hands in one of his, he took her in another fierce kiss. Their teeth banged, their tongues tangled, and he adeptly worked his button and zipper with one hand and pushed his pants down his thighs. She moaned, loud and urgent, struggling against his grip with the need to touch him.

"I've got you, baby." He pulled her skirt up to her waist and thrust his hand between her legs.

She was drenched, aching for his touch, his cock, his mouth. All of him.

"Fuck, baby. I wish I'd known you didn't have panties on." He stared into her eyes as he pushed his fingers into her, stroking the spot that made her insides burn. "I would have made you come the whole way here."

She couldn't stop a whimper from escaping. He claimed her in a demanding kiss. His talented fingers took her up, up, *up*. She trembled and gasped, her insides straining, reaching for the orgasm building within her. Then his thumb brushed over her clit in the most hypnotizing pattern, firm and soft, firm and soft. Rivers of heat surged through her. She came *hard*, crying out as she hit the peak. He drew back with a predatory stare, and without a word he dropped to his knees and pushed her legs apart so wide she had to grab his head to keep from falling over. His mouth covered her sex, sucking and teasing her to near madness.

"Please, Mick. I can't take it. Too…" *Oh God.*

His tongue entered her again and again. Threads of pleasure coursed down her legs, through her core, as another climax built, filling her veins, her limbs, and pulsing like a whip to the rhythm of his tongue. His mouth was relentless, taking and giving, making every nerve sizzle and burn. Her body flashed cold, then white-hot, and hotter still, until her mind was spinning, spinning, spinning—

"Mick!"

She arched off the door. A stream of pleas sailed from her lips, "Don't stop! More! There!" An explosion of sensations bled together, engulfing her in pleasure so exquisite it felt lethal.

Mick rose to his feet, and she slid lower on numb, useless legs, her back against the door. He lifted her in his arms and lowered her onto his shaft.

"Ohmygod." He filled her so perfectly, so completely, her head tipped back and the world careened away.

"You feel so good, baby."

Every thrust brought sparks of breath-stealing heat. She clawed at his shoulders, trying to match his efforts, but the orgasms had left her muscles weak, and it was all she could do to hold on tight.

"Harder," she pleaded.

Using the door for leverage, he pounded into her. On the verge of another climax, her inner muscles clenched *tight, tight, tight.* He tugged her mouth to his, kissing her hard and possessively, sending her spiraling into ecstasy. He was right there with her, grunting out her name as his release took hold—kissing, rocking, thrusting, until the last tremor rolled through them. He collapsed against her, still firm and buried deep. They were panting, half dressed, and covered in a sheen of sweat. She'd come so explosively, her body was still trying to catch up.

Mick drew back just enough to look deeply into her eyes, and she swore she saw eager affection looking back at her. "One weekend," he said, not unkindly.

"One weekend," she whispered.

He rested his cheek on her chest and she reveled in the luxurious feeling, being close to the man she adored. *One weekend.* She tried to make that thought stick, but it was like a fly circling, landing long enough for her to know it was there, but every breath, every blink, sent it circling again.

**

MICK KICKED OFF his jeans, still holding Amanda, warm and languid in his arms, and carried her through the living room.

"I can walk," she said groggily.

"I like this better."

She looked down at her clothes. Her shirt was wrinkled, damp with perspiration—his and hers—and open across her chest. Her skirt was still pushed up around her hips. She was delectable.

"You're pantsless and I'm fully dressed," she said with a humorous smile. "I like this."

"You're pantiless," he reminded her, "which makes you almost as naked as me, which I happen to like a whole hell of a lot, too."

Mick carried her through the master bedroom to the bathroom. Sunshine streamed in through a large picture window above the claw-foot tub, giving them a glorious view of the lake.

"Is this where we're staying tonight? It's really cute."

"Not nearly as cute as you, but no. I thought we'd stay on my boat." He set her down by the tub, keeping one arm around her waist to steady her. A sexually sated Amanda had quickly become one of his favorite things—a close second to the act of sexually satiating her. He'd never had a woman in this bathroom. The rough stone and dark wood walls made her seem even more delicate and feminine. He liked seeing her in his private oasis.

"You have a boat?" She rested her hand on his forearm. "You're just full of secrets, aren't you?"

"Apparently not around you." He took her in a long, unhurried kiss. It felt so good to let himself be close to her, to push aside the pretense and stress of pretending he didn't want her as *his*. She was his this weekend. "Let's wash up, and then I'll run down and get your things so you can change."

He began unbuttoning her shirt, and she covered his hand with hers. "You're going to stay?"

"You don't want to shower together?"

Her perfectly manicured brows knitted together. "I've never..."

Damn, she was going to kill him with sweetness. *At least it'll be an enjoyable death.* It floored him that she could be embarrassed by anything after all they'd done, but that was just one of the things that set her apart from other women and made Mick feel even more protective of her. He'd taken her roughly. Now he wanted to care for her.

"This isn't about sex," he assured her. "It's about treating you the way you deserve to be treated. Shower with me. Allow yourself to be pampered and cherished. Then we'll grab something to eat and go to the festival."

A wave of apprehension washed over her face, and it twisted his heart anew. He didn't want to push her any further past her comfort zone. He'd done that Friday night, and getting her to agree to spend this weekend together had been more of a shove than a push. "I'll wash up in the other bathroom and give you your privacy."

"No. Stay," she said with a sweet smile. "I'm curious about the pampering."

He was a hell of a lucky man. "Then let me satisfy that curiosity."

He slowly worked the buttons on her blouse, placing a single kiss between her breasts as he slipped it off her shoulders and set it aside.

"It's not about sex," he reassured her as he unhooked her bra, slid the cups from her breasts, and brushed his fingers over her nipples, loving the tiny gasp it earned. "It's about allowing me to take care of you," he whispered, and pressed a kiss to each taut peak.

He reached behind her and unzipped her skirt. It slid off her hips and puddled at her feet. He tugged his shirt over his head and tossed it aside. She placed a trembling hand on his forearm as he stepped closer, his hard cock pressed against her belly, his chest brushing hers.

"Are you okay, baby?"

She nodded, lips slightly parted, eyes wide. So beautiful he wished he could carry her to the bedroom and make love to her again, but this wasn't about sex. This was about releasing all the pent-up, unfamiliar desires he'd been trying to ignore.

He dropped to one knee, and she gripped his shoulders as he removed each of her boots, then gently massaged each foot.

She sighed. "That feels *incredible.*"

"Good, baby. I want you to feel good." The scent of her desire made his mouth water. Sliding his hands up her outer thighs, he rose one degree at a time and pressed a kiss to the cleft of her glistening sex.

His name sailed from her lips like a secret—"Mick"—and he forced himself to continue moving, slowing again to press a kiss just above her belly button and another to the swell of each breast. She was shaking, and he wasn't in much better shape, hard and desperate for more. But he'd made a promise, and he intended to keep it.

Gazing into her eyes, he wasn't surprised by the trust and shyness swimming in them. "You're beautiful, Amanda, and I know you're not used to having someone touch your body without an ulterior motive, but try to let yourself relax. Try to enjoy being touched and worshipped without the promise of sex hanging over you. As I said, this isn't about sex."

Her hand circled his erection. "Seems like it might be."

He smiled. "I'd love to bend you over the sink and take you from behind, baby. To sink into you and fuck you until"—*you never want another man*—"you're too spent and satiated to think."

Her breathing hitched, and her nails dug into his skin, making his struggle to hold back even tougher.

"We have plenty of time to play later. This is about cherishing you. I can't help it if my cock has other ideas." He brushed his thumb over her lower lip, then took her hand and guided her into the steamy shower. He stepped in behind her and gathered her hair over one shoulder to keep it from getting wet.

"Relax, baby. I've got you." He kissed her from shoulder to neck. "You're shaking. Are you cold?"

"No. Nervous."

He circled her waist with one arm and pressed his chest to her back. "I want to make you feel as special as you are. I've got you, baby." He held her beneath the warm shower as it rained down over her. "You're safe with me."

She exhaled, and he felt the tension in her muscles ease. He took his time washing her front first, neck, shoulders, and breasts, reveling in her tiny, desperate gasps as he moved over her nipples, down her belly to her mound, to her inner thighs. He lifted each arm, washing from wrist to shoulder and beneath. He lathered her with soapy hands, memorizing the dips and curves of her supple body, soaking in every tremble, every sigh. As the bubbles washed away, he sealed those newly cleaned areas with kisses. Moving behind her again, he pressed his chest to her back and reached over her shoulder, taking her in a long, sensual kiss. The position was purposeful, requiring each of them to strain if they wanted it enough. He liked heightening her pleasure, doing things she didn't expect, rousing sensations he didn't think she'd experienced before. Her skin was hot and slick. She ground her ass against his cock, driving him out of his mind. He ached to take this further, but he resisted, wanting her to feel precious and safe.

"We have all day, baby," he assured her. "Anticipation is half the fun. Let me take care of you. Just relax and enjoy the ride." She whimpered, and he kissed her again, then released her face, focusing on her sleek backside again.

He crouched on the shower floor, washing her feet, ankles, and calves, and kissing each set of freckles as he discovered them—behind her knee, down the center of the back of her thigh. He loved knowing where her unique markings were. More secrets. He massaged her thighs as the bubbles washed away, earning another sweet whimper. She was killing him. He caressed the curve of her ass, kissing each firm globe as they rinsed clean.

"You're driving me crazy," she pleaded.

"Sorry, baby," he said with a gratified smile. He loved knowing the effect he had on her. He ran his finger down the crease between her cheeks, teasing her tightest hole and gauging her reaction. Her deep moan was all the invitation he needed to take it a little further, though he had no intention of going past bringing her new and exciting pleasures. Spreading her cheeks, he ran his tongue from the top of the crease all the way to her hole and circled the rim.

"Ohmygod." She thrust her ass out and reached for the wall. The visual was almost too much to take, her perfect ass hiked up, her legs slightly spread, and her glorious body on full display.

"Don't stop," she begged.

He hadn't realized he'd paused to drink in the erotic sight of her. He teased and licked in time to her rocking hips, sinking lower as she widened her stance. He couldn't resist tasting her slick heat. *Sweet as honey.* He licked from one entrance to the other, lingering on each.

"Again," she pleaded.

My pleasure. He did it again, and she moaned louder, more tortured.

"Baby, those sounds. You're seriously testing my control."

"Don't stop. Please don't stop," she said breathlessly.

Rising to his feet, he pressed his chest to her back again, moving them both toward the wall.

"This isn't supposed to be about sex," he said harshly, though he was talking to himself. "You're worth more than sex, Amanda. You need to know that." He reached around her and pressed his hand over her heart. "In here, where it counts. You need to know you're not just a pretty girl to fuck."

"I know that when I'm with you."

When I'm with you. "God, baby, what you do to me." He lowered his forehead to her shoulder as she ground her ass against him.

"Just...Do what you were doing. Lick me *there*."

He was pushing his limits on restraint. He should have known their connection was too deep, their fire burned too hot, to draw such a thin line between how far he'd go and how far he *wanted* to go.

Thrusting her ass against him again, she said, "Please?" in an excruciatingly innocent voice.

No fantasy could come close to the woman he adored giving herself so freely to him. And she was no longer his fantasy. She was here now. *His* for the weekend. She widened her legs, and he gave her what she wanted, licking and teasing, until she was panting and whimpering and he was on the verge of losing it. He thrust his tongue into her ass, and she cried out in sweet anguish.

"Touch yourself," he commanded. There was no turning back now. He had to make her come, had to feel her body shudder and shake.

Her hand dropped to her thigh, and he covered it with his own, moving it between her legs and pressing her fingers into her slick heat.

"That's it, baby. Feel that? That's what I do to you." He fisted his cock and pumped as he licked her ass and she fingered herself. "I could watch you and eat you all day long. I'm so hard. So fucking hard for you."

She stilled. The sound of the water and their heavy breathing mixed with the sound of flesh on flesh as he stroked his cock.

"Take me," she said shakily.

His hand stilled.

"*There.*"

He closed his eyes against the tentative demand in her sweet voice. "Amanda." He didn't mean to growl, but there was only so much he could take before he gave in.

"Please," she whispered. "I've never..."

Christ. Another first. A *huge* first. "Baby..."

She turned and faced him with fierce determination. "I thought this was *my* weekend."

"It is, but—"

She pushed the fingers that had been between her legs into his mouth, filling him with her essence, and he sucked them clean. Fear stormed inside him—of the emotions she was unearthing and the rampant desire she'd unleashed. He hadn't meant for this to lead to sex, but hell, he was only human.

"Christ, baby," he pleaded. "You can't undo this."

"I know I'll never feel this safe again, and I want to experience everything, Mick. With *you*. I trust you."

Her eyes pleaded as fervently as her words, shattering his last shred of control. He crashed his mouth over hers, taking her in a punishingly intense kiss.

"I don't want to hurt you," he said between kisses.

"I know you won't. I trust you."

He was as good as gone, and he had a feeling Monday would bring a world of hurt no matter how many times he warned her—or himself. "You're sure? Come Monday, you'll feel this every time you look at me."

She searched his face, but he had the distinct impression she wasn't registering it at all—she'd gone introspective, soul searching.

"I'm more than sure, Mick." She went up on her toes and pressed her lips to his, then turned around, and braced her hands against the wall.

Holy hell. He knew he'd see this image for the rest of his life. He kissed her spine, the back of her neck, her shoulders. His hands traveled south, and he dipped his fingers into her pussy, drenching them with her desire before touching them to the place she was offering. "I'm going to ease in, to get you ready, baby. If it hurts, we'll stop."

She nodded.

He slid one finger past the tight rim of muscles, and she gasped. "Too much?"

"No. *More.*"

He'd probably be struck by a truck for allowing himself to do this when he knew he couldn't give her the relationship she really wanted. But this was their weekend, and he wasn't about to deny either of them the pleasures they craved. He pushed two fingers in and her ass clenched tight. She moaned, her fingers clawing at the wall. He leaned forward, covering her hand with his and interlacing their fingers.

"I've got you, baby." He worked her ass until she moved with him more comfortably, meeting each inward thrust with a rock of her hips. "That's it, baby. We can stop at any time." He kissed her neck, grazed his teeth over her shoulder, and her breathing went from tenuous to lust-filled, fast and eager. "You run this show, baby. Tell me when you're ready."

She rested her head back against his shoulder. "I'm ready."

He withdrew carefully, washing his hand before guiding his cock into her center, earning another sharp gasp. "Just for a minute, baby. Lubrication."

Her pussy was so tight from the ass play he could have stayed buried there for the rest of the day. But she was giving him a gift, a chance to be closer to her than he'd ever imagined, and he wanted that more than he wanted his next breath. The warm water rained over them as he withdrew from between her legs and positioned the head of his cock at her tighter entrance. Her fingers curled around his as he pushed into her viselike channel. She sucked in a sharp breath.

"Too much?"

"Yes," she said, and he stilled. "No. Keep going."

He pushed in deeper, and she cried out. He froze, half buried. "We'll stop."

"No! Keep going," she panted out.

He wrapped his other hand around her waist and drove in with one fast thrust, until he was buried to the hilt.

"Ow, ow! Don't stop. Don't stop."

It killed him to hear pain tangled with the desire in her voice, and for a beat, he remained still.

"Please don't stop, Mick."

"Okay, baby. I hate to hurt you." He kissed the back of her neck, and she pressed back.

"I know," she said. "Don't stop."

He moved slowly, giving her the chance to get used to the fullness, the burn. "Still with me?"

"Yes. Yes, so good."

"That's right, baby. You feel so good, and I'm going to make you feel even better." He moved his hand from her waist to between her legs.

"Oh Lord," she said in a heady voice. "That's...Wow. The pain."

Mick stilled again, gutted. "Amanda—"

Her head fell between her shoulders. "Don't stop. I didn't expect to *like* it."

Relief and something much bigger, much more meaningful, enveloped him. He refused to name the emotions, but he allowed himself to feel and acknowledge their overwhelming presence.

"Good, baby. Now let's make you come."

He reveled in the sweet sounds of surrender streaming from her lips as she came and the explosiveness of his relief as he followed her over the edge. Wrapping his arms around her middle, kissing her cheek, her shoulder, her neck, anywhere he could reach, he reassured her, told her how incredible she was. He wanted all of her, heart and soul, but he was a prisoner to his conscience. She wasn't *his* beyond this weekend, and thinking she could ever be set them both up for a world of hurt. He crammed the possessive thought down beneath his desire, beneath the emptiness that had been his companion for far too long, to a well of unending darkness.

If only he had a cap and chains to keep it there.

Chapter Nine

THE FALL FESTIVAL was in full swing when Mick and Amanda finally made it to the fairgrounds. Colorful balloons waved from the corner posts of big white tents, like confetti that had been tossed from the sky. A cool breeze swept off the lake, carrying sounds of families frolicking by the shore and festivalgoers laughing and talking, eating ice cream, cupcakes, and pink blooms of cotton candy. Giggling teenage girls huddled together, eyeing surly and cocky boys, full of life and the indestructability of youth. Amanda had expected to be hugely embarrassed after what they'd done in the shower, but all through lunch she'd waited for mortification to hit, and it never did. She was as relieved as she was baffled. How could being with him feel so right and still be temporary?

They meandered through tents, marveling at arts and crafts and listening to music coming from the bandstand. She was fully entrenched in the fantasy he'd created for her, bringing her into this gorgeous small town, into the safety of his arms, and allowing her to explore parts of herself she'd never imagined *wanting* to explore. With Mick, it felt natural to want to experience every sensation she possibly could, to be as close as two people could get. He was a feast for her body, her brain, *and* her heart, regardless of the confines he'd drawn around them. And even more of a mystery to her now than when he'd worn a mask. He was tender and kind, yet visceral and, at times, slightly controlling. She'd noticed that along with his more aggressive side came a thoughtful tenderness, checking in with her often to ensure she was okay, and it was an entrancing combination. Like a sleek and powerful panther exposing its soft underbelly. He'd fulfilled his promise of pampering her after he'd finished satisfying her surprising naughty desires. He'd lavished her with kisses, soothed her with reassurances and compliments as sweet as candy, and washed her so lovingly, she didn't know how he was going to pretend any better than she would be able to on Monday.

Mick tightened his arm around her and pressed his lips to her temple, drawing her toward another tent. Above the entrance, a gold banner with *La Love* written in black script across the center waved in the breeze.

"Hi, y'all. Welcome to La Love," a pretty brunette said from behind a jewelry display. She did a double take when she saw Amanda. "I love your sweater. Where'd you get it? At Misty's? I heard she's got a whole new fall lineup, but I haven't had the time to stop in and see it for myself."

Amanda had worn jeans and a wide-necked peach silk sweater. The neckline rode the edge of her shoulders, which Mick said made it *luxurious and sexy*.

"Thank you. I've never been to Misty's. I'm from New York City, and I picked this up at Filene's Basement." She held her arm out. "Feel how soft it is. It was a steal at seventy percent off."

The woman touched it and smiled. "Mm. Isn't that just delicious?" She smiled at Mick, who was peering intently at a display of necklaces. "Bet he thinks so, too."

Mick shifted devilishly dark eyes to Amanda. "She is very delicious."

She felt her cheeks heat up and busied herself by perusing the earrings. She was trying really hard not to read too much into the things he said and did, but how was she supposed to not read into *that*?

"Y'all are too cute. I'm Heaven. Heaven Love," the brunette said.

"I'm Amanda, and this is Mick. That's a great name, by the way."

"Thanks to the seventies, our mama gave us all colorful names." Heaven shrugged. "Are you in town for the festival, or did you come for a lover's weekend and get lucky?"

Mick reached for her hand, and she knew he was going to say something that would make her blush. She gave him her best *don't you dare* look.

His expression turned from mischievous to...*adoring*?

She needed air. Lots of it. Maybe an oxygen mask or an oxygen chamber. That might do it. She pointed to the community rec center across the grounds. "I'm going to use the ladies' room. I'll be right back."

"I'll walk you over," Mick offered.

"No! I mean, thanks, but it's okay. I'll be right

back." She hurried out of the tent, drew in a lungful of air, and made a beeline for the ladies' room.

Pushing through the doors, she pulled her phone from her pocket and called Ally. *Pick up. Pick up.*

"So?" Ally answered.

"So, I need your advice. I think I've royally messed up."

"You never royally mess up. You *trip*. *I* fall ass over teakettle."

"Yeah?" Amanda laughed. "Well, guess what? My ass has taken a pounding." *Literally.* "Al, can I tell you something without you telling Heath?"

"I'm your sister. You can tell me anything."

Amanda cringed as she said, "I'm with Mick."

"As in *your boss*? He's your mystery man?"

"Mm-hm. We have an agreement. Just this weekend and we'll never speak of it again. I thought— *I think*—I can do it. But I need some help. I'm seeing things that aren't there. Looks. Reading more into them, into the things he says. How do you avoid that?" Except maybe they *were* real. He said he wanted her. *For the weekend.*

Ugh! She was so confused!

"You don't sleep with the man you've wanted for, oh, I don't know, *three* flipping years!"

"I know, I know, I know." She paced, knowing she was in too deep to ever *not* see a single thing. But she could try. She had to try. "But I'm *way* past that. Just tell me how. That's all I need."

"God, Mandy. What about your job? This isn't like you. No wonder you didn't tell me. I would have handcuffed you for sure."

"I know. Ally, please? Don't judge me. Just tell me how to get these rose-colored glasses off."

"There are a few surefire ways to keep your head on straight, but none of them will work for you, because you're sleeping with the guy you *want*." She yelled the word *want*. "Never again do I let you try anything risky on your own."

"But the book said—"

"The book?" Ally yelled. "Burn that stupid book. This is my fault. I should have been with you every step of the way."

"That would have been awkward in the shower when we were—"

"Stop!" Ally laughed. "Okay, look. You're all about reasonable and rational thinking, so take that route."

"Yeah, that pretty much went out the window the second we kissed, so do you have anything else up your sleeve? Magic pills that will turn me into a cold, unfeeling tramp or something?"

"God, Mandy. You really have gone ass over teakettle."

"No shit, sis. Help?"

"No tramp potions, but there's the obvious thing that I'm sure you've already considered. You'll lose your job if you can't control yourself. Jesus, how are you going to work with him?"

"I've worked with him for three years and wanted him practically that whole time, so what's the difference?"

Ally sighed. "You can't play a player."

Her sister saw right through her. "I know. The truth is, I've already pretty much decided that I have to quit my job."

"Aw, Mandy," Ally said empathetically. "I wish I knew how to help, but you're crossing lines I never did."

"So, no secrets for me, then? I'm on my own?"

"I think I'm in shock. You're not on your own. I'm here for you, but I'll have to think on how to handle this."

She knew that would be the case, but she felt better coming clean to Ally and hearing her say she'd be there for her when she fell apart—which she would when they were back in the real world again.

"Okay. I have to go. I left him out there and took off like a bat out of hell."

"Wait!" Ally said. "I've got it. Remember when Mom and Dad caught us sneaking out over your sophomore year when you *had* to see that dork, what's his name?"

Amanda smiled with the memory. "Martin. I remember. *Pinchigans?* You think it'll work?"

"It wiped that smart-ass smile off your face every time."

"Genius, Al. Sorry I didn't tell you about Mick."

"That's okay. At least I know he'd never physically hurt you, which, by the way, I'm going to do when I see you Monday night, so be ready."

"Love you, too, sis." She ended the call, thinking about Ally's suggestion.

Pinchigans. Every time their parents caught them sneaking out to see Martin, she'd smile, because he was cute and funny and sneaking out was exciting. But her smile gave her away, and her parents knew their story about taking a walk in the moonlight had been a lie—every single time. Ally began giving Amanda a little pinch whenever they'd get caught, just hard enough to snap her mind back to reality, giving them time to formulate new excuses. *Perfect.*

She pulled open the bathroom door and headed

for the jewelry tent in search of Mick.

"Amanda!"

She turned toward Mick's voice, and her heart nearly stopped at the sight of him carrying a small boy on his shoulders. One arm curled up around the little boy's bottom, and the other was draped over a very attractive blonde's shoulder. The blonde was smiling up at the boy. They could have walked right out of *Family Circle* magazine, if not for the fact that Mick's eyes were locked on Amanda—with that look she was sure was born from her hopes and dreams and all things sinful.

She didn't know who the woman and child were, and she should have been swamped with jealousy, but *that look* stood in the way. It rooted itself into her heart, the warmth of it spreading like limbs into her mind. She managed a half smile, half oh-shit stare, drew her hands behind her back, and put her Get My Head On Straight Plan into action.

Pinchigan. Pinchigan. Pinchigan.

**

A KNOT ROSE in Mick's throat as he and Bridgette approached Amanda. When Amanda had run off to the bathroom, he'd worried it all had become too much for her—their intimacy, his comments, which were meant to send a secret, sexy message. Now her eyes were guarded, bringing more disquieting thoughts.

"Who's that?" Bridgette's four-year-old son, Louie, asked from atop Mick's shoulders, reminding Mick that Amanda had no idea who his friends were.

Could she be jealous? That brought a real smile.

"That's my friend Amanda," he said to Louie. He'd

never called her *his friend* before. With colleagues he referred to her as his *paralegal* or *employee*, either of which was safe. With Willow he hadn't labeled her but had defined their relationship as that of research partners. Those tags defined a degree of separation that, until yesterday, he'd respected, and they had helped keep him in check. But none of those descriptions fit her this weekend, and *friend* didn't even begin to describe his feelings toward her.

Bridgette leaned closer to him. "Friend? Not according to Willow. She's stunning, by the way."

Yeah, he knew. Stunning, sweet, charming, smart, sensual. Hell, if he believed in forever, he'd add *permanently his* to that list. But seeing Bridgette and Louie only reinforced that forever was a fantasy. Bridgette had lost the love of her life, her first and only love, Louie's father, when Louie was just a baby.

"Hi, 'Manda! I'm Louie."

Amanda's guarded expression softened, and she smiled up at Louie. "Hi. Are you having fun up there?"

Louie laughed. "Yes! I'm riding the Mick train!"

The blush rising on Amanda's cheeks told Mick she was thinking about how she'd already enjoyed that ride, the same way he was. Maybe it was jealousy he'd seen after all.

"Amanda, this is Bridgette, Willow's sister. Louie is Bridgette's son."

"Hi," Amanda said. "It's nice to meet you both."

Bridgette embraced her. "Willow said she ran into you guys earlier, and the minute Louie heard Mick was here, he *had* to find him." She reached her arms up toward Louie. "Come on, buddy. Let's go get a cupcake from Auntie Willow."

Mick lifted Louie from his shoulders, and the little

boy threw his arms around his neck.

"Will I see you before you go home?"

"I'm not sure, buddy." Mick hugged him tight, catching the dreaminess on Amanda's face, stirring all those conflicting emotions again. "But I brought you a little something."

Louie grabbed Mick's cheeks and pressed his tiny lips to his. "Thank you!"

They all laughed.

"You don't even know what it is yet."

"It doesn't matter. Mom says we thank people for thinking of us." Louie smiled at Bridgette, then said, "Logan brings me baseball cards, so he gets extra thank-yous."

Mick set Louie on the ground, meeting Bridgette's heartrending smile. Her husband had collected baseball cards, and she'd been deeply touched when Logan began bringing them for Louie. But that was Logan and Louie's *thing*, and while Mick loved bringing gifts for his little buddy, he'd never step on Logan's toes.

He pulled a harmonica from his back pocket and handed it to Louie. "This might not be as good as baseball cards, but hopefully you'll have some fun with it."

Louie jumped up and down and threw his arms around Mick's legs. "Thank you, thank you, thank you!"

Amanda's eyes filled with something sweet and maternal. He crouched to avoid the emotions that stirred and showed Louie how to use his new toy.

"You would make a great dad," Bridgette said emphatically.

"Bridge," Mick warned. They'd been through this. She knew he'd sworn off having a family, but she never failed to point out how great a father he'd make. He'd had a great father once, and he'd watched that man turn into anything but. The apple didn't fall far from the tree, and he wasn't about to put himself, or anyone else, through that type of nightmare.

Bridgette rolled her eyes.

Amanda's brows knitted.

"We'd better go for real this time, before a certain little person decides he needs more of M-I-C-K." Bridgette hugged Amanda. "It was nice to meet you. I hope we see you again sometime."

"I'm glad we had a chance to meet." Amanda turned to Louie, who was spinning in circles while blowing into his harmonica. "Have fun making music, Louie."

"I will!" he yelled as his mother took his hand and they headed toward the tents.

"Talk about cute!" Amanda exclaimed. "Where did you get the harmonica?"

"I always bring him a little something. I picked it up when we stopped for gas on the way here." He took her hand. Despite her wide smile and bright eyes, he was still thinking about the uneasy look he'd seen earlier, and he needed to know if she was feeling regrets.

"You didn't look happy earlier," he said cautiously. "Are you having second thoughts? Do you want to talk about what we did? About anything?"

She shook her head, but the uneasy expression returned. He stepped closer and she looked down. He curled a finger under her chin, lifting her beautiful face.

"What we did was intense, and not at all planned. If we crossed too many lines, you need to tell me."

Her hands slid from his to behind her back. "I asked you to do it."

"Baby, what we say in the heat of the moment, when everything feels right, can feel completely different afterward. If that's the case, you need to tell me. I might be your sex toy for the weekend, but there are no batteries to take out to turn me off. I have a mind of my own, and if I know you don't like, or regret, anything, I'll know better how to handle other things." He brushed his thumb over her cheek, and a smile lifted her lips. "You do crazy stuff to my dirty mind, so it's important that we trust each other. I need to know how you honestly feel."

Her eyes went glassy, filling him with a foreboding ache.

"Amanda?"

"Hm?"

"You look like you're going to cry." He folded her in his arms. "Shit, baby. I'm sorry. I should have known it was too much."

She pushed out of his arms with a frustrated exhalation. "I'm *not* going to cry, and it wasn't too much. I just scratched my arm by accident."

Scratched your arm? A small pink mark had appeared on her arm. "You're sure?"

"Yes," she snapped. "I'm fine with what we did. I liked it. Hell, Mick, I *loved* it. I'm just processing everything. You. Me. What we did. What we're doing. The craziness going on inside me."

He pushed a hand through his hair, watching her watch him. She crossed her arms and leveled him with a serious stare. A seriously *hot* stare. He felt his lips quirk up, and hers did the same, the playful look rattling his heart.

"I don't know what to make of that." He laughed.

Her smile widened. "Think I do?"

"Not if I'm reading you right, but you're seriously messing with my head." He tugged her in close again, and she wound her arms around his neck, laughing softly. The sweet melody made his head spin even more. "I should strip you bare and take you right here, just for messing with me."

"Oh, no." Her voice turned serious. "Are you one of those, what do you call them? Those men who like to punish girls?"

"*Jesus.* Do I *seem* like one of those guys?"

"How should I know? You're the teacher. I'm merely the student."

"You're not *merely* anything. And you're no student, Amanda. I don't know what you are, but it's not that." He pressed his lips to hers in a chaste kiss. "To answer your question, no, I'm not a dom, but I'd be happy to spank you if you're into that sort of thing." He waggled his brows.

"I bet you would."

She had him so tied in knots, he wasn't sure he was reading anything right, making it even more important to clarify where her head was. "How's the processing going? Do you want to change gears and scale it back? Spend the rest of the weekend as friends?"

"You told Bridgette and Louie we were friends. I don't see the difference, Counselor." The defiance in her voice was new and thrilling.

"Well, then..." He draped an arm over her shoulder, liking the feel of her so much he decided she belonged there. At least for the weekend. "Let me rephrase the question. Do you still want to fuck or not?"

"Oh, that's what you meant?" Feigned innocence coated every word. "Affirmative. That is, unless some other hot guy piques my interest at the bar tonight."

Jealousy gnawed at him. "Is that the game we're playing now?"

"A girl has to keep her options open. And did you miss the part where I called you hot? Geez, your listening skills leave a little to be desired. You obviously didn't have the best teacher."

"Careful. You're turning me on with your smart-assery." Everything she did was turning him on and turning him inside out in equal measure. He needed to lighten his thoughts, and headed for the parking lot instead of the festival. "What do you say we blow off the festival and take my motorcycle out for a spin?"

"You have a motorcycle? I don't remember hearing about this during the initial questioning," she teased. "My boss warned me about slippery lawyers like you."

He probably should have warned *himself* about *her*, because the more time they spent together, the more he wished Monday would never come.

Chapter Ten

MICK DIDN'T JUST have a motorcycle. He had a shiny, black Indian motorcycle. The name didn't mean squat to Amanda, but watching Mick straddling the powerful machine was the sexiest thing she'd ever seen. She loved the feel of his muscles flexing and the heat searing through his back as she clung to him on the ride up the mountain. The roar of the bike filled her with adrenaline. The crisp evening air was as shocking as it was thrilling, seeping through her sweater to the skin beneath. Riding on the back of the motorcycle made the whole world look different. The trees seemed brighter, the smells were sharper, and the asphalt was no longer just a road but a path to freedom. Amanda felt untethered but not reckless, which she attributed to Mick. He was careful with her, grounding her, going over the rules of the road and secret signals in case she got scared. He drove like he owned the road, *owned* the very earth beneath them.

He veered off the main drag onto a narrow road

that was more like a trail, buffered by woods. The sun was just beginning to set, casting a bluish hue through the thick umbrella of trees. The scent of pine and raw earth filled her lungs. The bike slowed as they neared the edge of the woods. Amanda's insides hummed long after he cut the engine.

It took a few minutes for the roar of the bike to silence in her head, allowing the sounds of the forest to filter in. Branches swished overhead; leaves swirled along the grass and dirt. Mick climbed off the bike and removed his helmet. He shook out his hair, and Amanda felt like she was watching a scene from a movie made just for her. *Mick Bad, Super Hottie.* His lips curved into a delicious smile as he dug his cell phone from his pocket. His whiskers had thickened throughout the evening, and he looked even more like he had the night of the bar crawl. The more time they spent together outside the office, the harder it became to picture him in his suit and tie, with his mask of professionalism firmly in place.

He held up his phone. "You look hot. I want one picture of you on my bike."

"Wait." She reached for her helmet, trying to pry it off, and he stopped her with a thoughtful gleam in his eyes. He lowered her hand and took the picture.

"Our little secret," he promised. He helped her take off the helmet and lifted her from the bike like a hundred and twenty-five pounds was nothing.

She liked knowing he wanted to have something to remember their time together. It gave her the freedom to ask for the same.

"Can I take a picture of you so I have one, too?"

He tugged her against his side and held his phone out for a selfie of the two of them. "Say cheese, baby."

He kissed her cheek as he took the picture. She turned and he kissed her lips, taking another few pictures, which she was sure caught her in a number of shocked and delighted expressions.

Her heart turned over in her chest. She was, for the first time in a very long time, truly happy with a man. She didn't want to worry about later, or tomorrow, or Monday. She just wanted to revel in what they had now, and hope it lasted forever.

"I'll text you copies. Come on. I want to show you something." He took her hand and they walked across a clearing to an overlook. Rocky hills dotted with thick tufts of trees mapped the cascading mountainside. Sweetwater was nestled in a valley below. The lake reflected the setting sun like black glass, and roads snaked through the small town, disappearing beyond the peaks and valleys. She thought of the city's smoggy air filled with pungent smells of exhaust and grime and the aggressive, overwhelming sounds of too many people.

She inhaled the fresh mountain air and sank down to the grass beside Mick.

He motioned to the incredible view. "Your postcard view of Sweetwater."

She wondered if he used the word *postcard* because she had on their way into town, or if it was a coincidence. He rested his hand on her leg and smiled. His thoughtful gaze held her answer. She couldn't imagine anything more perfect than sharing this incredibly picturesque moment with him. When he put an arm around her, it felt natural to rest her head against him.

"You have a nice life here. Willow and Bridgette seem wonderful, and Louie is adorable. Do you come often?"

He chuckled, and she bumped him with her shoulder.

"You're such a guy. I didn't mean the double entendre."

"I don't come as often as I'd like," he said. "Pun intended." He held his phone up and took another picture of them, then turned it toward the view and clicked off a few more shots.

He began texting the pictures to her, and she mulled him over: the man, the attorney, the mystery.

"What if you get a nosy girlfriend?" she asked, admittedly fishing for clues to his firm stance on relationships. "Aren't you worried someone might see those?"

He shoved his phone into his pocket and stared out at the sunset. "Not going to happen."

"Why? You're hotter than any actor, a brilliant attorney, and a badass motorcycle-driving sex machine. Your female clients dress like they'd do you in the office. Why would you cut yourself off from finding *the one*?"

He chuckled. "A badass motorcycle-driving sex machine?"

The fact that he didn't take the bait did not go unnoticed. "Not that I want to inflate your ego or anything, but yes."

"Thanks, baby, but I'm not into relationships. I told you that." He looked out at the sunset again.

She wasn't giving up that easily. "Why?"

"I could ask you the same thing," he said casually.

"I want a relationship." She leaned back on her palms and sighed. "I want it all. A job I enjoy, a *man* I enjoy. A life that's stable and interesting, sexy and fun.

I want to look at my husband and know, without a shadow of a doubt, that I'm the one he wants. The *only* one, no matter what."

She sat up and crossed her legs, realizing she was telling him the honest to goodness truth without worrying about what he thought of her because of it and decided to spill it all. She plucked a few blades of grass, suddenly nervous at the prospect.

"I want a man who loves me enough to stand on the road with a boom box for all the world to see, or show up at my door with signs proclaiming his love."

"John Cusack and Andrew Lincoln. You want romantic-movie love."

"I can't believe you know that. I didn't peg you for a guy who watched romantic movies."

"I've never seen them, but you'd have to live in a cave not to have heard about those scenes."

He drew his knees up and rested his forearms on them, staring straight ahead, his brows knitted. Amanda had always been fascinated by the way his mind worked, and she recognized the way his eyes narrowed, his jaw tightened, and the air around him beat with deep concentration. He'd slipped into attorney mode. In the courtroom, this was the mask he wore in the moments between knowing his next step and changing it up to win a case. He called those contemplative silences his *ascendance*. Other attorneys stuck to their scripts. They planned strategies and rode them out. Mick was as fluid in the courtroom as he was in the bedroom, forgoing his plan to find the right path, the right angle, *the right touch*, to secure his win. Knowing that about him brought a smile, but that smile didn't last long, because soon she'd no longer see him in the courtroom, the office, or at all.

"Movie romance is your thing," he said absently, "and you should have it."

"Before Ally met Heath, she used to tease me about wanting that. She said it wasn't real, but now she believes in true love."

"I didn't know that about her." He turned with a serious expression. "Why didn't she believe in love?"

Amanda shrugged. "You know about her being hurt. One of my *sad* moments," she reminded him. "That broke her, and I guess no one could heal that break until Heath."

"Why do you think? Why Heath? He's an awesome dude, but what was it about him?" His tone was reminiscent of an inquisition, and she wondered why he was so curious.

"I think Heath was just what she needed at that time of her life. He *got* her. Neither of them were into relationships, and somehow he made her feel safe and sexy and happy, and she made him feel..." It was one thing to share her own feelings, but she realized it wasn't right to share Ally's.

"I think when you *click*, when you find *the one*, you know it, and Ally knew it right away." *I've known for a very long time, but now I'm even more sure. And equally as sure that telling you so would be perilous.*

He shifted his eyes away again, nodding as if he agreed.

"And you? Why don't you see a relationship in your future?" She plucked a few more pieces of grass and shredded them.

He scoffed. "I'm with the old Ally. Love is a fantasy. That's why they make movies about it, because real life isn't like that." He eyed her curiously. "For most people, anyway. I hope you find it."

She was beginning to see a correlation between Mick and Ally's previous beliefs, but she wasn't sure why, and she wondered if he'd had his heart broken by a woman in the past. Although she wasn't about to ask him. Instead, she debated his belief.

"My parents have been married forever, and I think they're truly happy."

"You know the divorce rates. Life, love, work. Everything's transient. Everything changes."

"But..." *But what? I want you to want a relationship?* That was the stupidest thing she could say, because people didn't change. Only her sister and Heath were proof that they could, and according to Mick, everything changed. It was still a stupid thing to say, like poking a bear.

"How about your parents?" she asked. "Are they still together?"

"Not even close." He kicked his legs out, crossed them, and leaned back on his hands. Worry lines crept across his forehead.

"I'm sorry. I didn't know."

"It's better this way."

"Why? Did they fight a lot?"

He sat up again, clearly agitated. She expected him to tell her he was done with this conversation.

"Not at first," he admitted. "But life has a way of tearing people apart."

She could tell by the tension in his jaw that he was reaching his limit, but she'd come this far. She wasn't about to let it go without saying her piece.

"Sure it does, but you fight through it if you love each other. There's always good with bad. That's what makes a relationship, isn't it? It can't be good all the time. That's the difference between love and infatuation. Love lasts. Infatuation is transient."

**

MICK TRIED TO temper the frustration that followed thoughts of his youth, but his emotions were all over the place. He felt like a twig, perched to snap beneath the weight of a grizzly.

"You're naive," he said too roughly. "I never pegged you as naive."

Amanda sat up straighter. "I'm not naive, and that's not a very nice thing to say."

"I'm not trying to be mean, Amanda. But you've lived a perfect life, with a family who adores you. Mom, Dad, and two perfect girls. Life isn't like that for everyone."

"We're hardly the perfect family, but even so, people without perfect lives still fall in love. Look at Heath and Ally. Heath's father was murdered. His mother beaten and blinded. That's not perfect, and he loves Ally to the ends of the earth. I believe love can last, and I believe it can conquer anything, even if it sounds naive."

He gritted his teeth against the truth, but it came out anyway. "And Heath's parents? His mother lost the man she adored. Nothing lasts. We all die, and death changes those left behind."

She inched closer when she should have been running in the opposite direction, looking at him with so much compassion he felt it surrounding him. His insides coiled tight, fighting against her efforts to get him to open up to her—and his heart warred for a chance at what he'd never had or wanted before.

"Did you lose someone you loved?" she asked.

Fuck. This was not something he wanted to talk about. He turned away, hoping she'd take the hint. She moved even closer, their bodies joined at the hip, thigh, and shoulder, but she said nothing. She didn't have to. Compassion and worry rolled off of her and stroked over him like a caress. A cacophony of nature filled the silence as they lost themselves in the setting sun. Minutes passed, ten, twenty? He wasn't sure how long, but it was enough time for him to realize she'd eased the pressure in his chest simply by remaining at his side.

He reached for her hand. It was so small and delicate he could hide it in his own. She was delicate, and yet she was stronger than he was, putting her heart on the line. She'd already given herself to him in so many ways, and now she was giving him even more, and in turn, she'd earned something he hadn't known was up for grabs—his trust.

He tucked a strand of hair behind her ear and stroked her cheek. For the first time in his life, he wanted to share his past. He'd run from it for so long that he wasn't even sure how to talk about it, but when he looked at Amanda, his heart knew.

"We lost our sister, Lorelei, to leukemia when she was eight." He hadn't said her name aloud in so many years, he wanted to cradle it in his arms and keep it safe. "I was fourteen."

Amanda's eyes dampened. "I'm so sorry. I can't imagine..."

He cleared his throat to speak past the emotions clogging it. "I haven't told many people that. Heath's family knows because we grew up together, and the Daltons know. When Bridgette's husband was killed, we all helped her through. But I haven't shared it with anyone else."

"Thank you for trusting me, and I'm sorry for Bridgette and Louie. I didn't know she'd lost her husband." She pressed her lips to his in a kiss so sweet and warm he wanted to climb inside it and hole up for the night. "It's okay if you don't want to talk about it."

"I don't know what I want, but this feels good. Talking to you feels good. We never talk about her. None of us do." Mick scrubbed a hand down his face, trying to regain control of his emotions. "Before we lost her, we were a big, loud, loving family. Family dinners, four hellion boys with a sister to protect. We knew who we were. Then Lorelei got sick, and it all changed so fast. She'd been tired for a while, but then she got worse. The flu, my parents thought. She went downhill quickly. She got really weak, bloody noses, pain. God, it was like she hurt all over. Then the diagnosis came, and chemo, more tests. One day she had this rash and my mom was taking her to a doctor, and it seemed like the next we were sitting vigil by her hospital bed. Then the lights went out."

His chest constricted with each memory, but he continued revealing one after another, because as painful as it was to talk about, it was equally as freeing. He'd kept his secret, as though his sister's cancer fed off of it, taking him down with her, which he felt like he deserved, so he'd continued feeding it year after year.

"We lost her," he choked out. "And we each lost a piece of ourselves. My mother cried day and night. My father buried himself in work, and my brothers and I did what kids do when parents lose their grip. We turned that sadness inward, and it ate us up. We couldn't talk about it, because we were afraid of our parents hearing or of crying—and we were what? Ten to fourteen? Not great ages for dealing with anything, especially tears. Better to man up and bury the pain."

She squeezed his hand, bringing his eyes to hers again and drawing more of his past from the depths of his soul.

"One day I guess our parents could no longer stand the silence, and their relationship erupted. That was all it took for the rest of us to fall apart. We each handled it differently. Dylan's anger only lasted a few weeks, but losing our sister changed him. He used to be the kid who could make anyone laugh. Carefree, everyone's friend. He became colder, less trusting, raised some hell with Heath and his brothers; we all did. Carson wasn't as bad as the rest of us. You know how even-keeled he is. He was careful not to get into too much trouble, and he holed up in his bedroom for a year. That was the year he learned to hack computers. And Brett?"

He shook his head, surprised at how much he was sharing and how it didn't feel like he was ripping his guts out, as it had when he'd shared it with the Daltons.

"Brett was closest in age to Lorelei. She looked up to all of us, but we played different roles in her life, like siblings do. Lorelei had a calming effect on Brett. Afterward, he became surly, and as he got older, that surliness turned to rage."

He realized Amanda had that same calming effect on him. Thinking about their connection, he turned away, taking in ribbons of purple and blue streaming across the sky, the remnants of the sun as it dipped behind the mountains. Amanda fed his emotions like the sun fed flowers, and he felt himself reaching for her more and more, craving her light.

"And you?" she asked.

"I'm the eldest. The protector. I got my brothers out of the house when my parents fought, slept with one ear open in case they needed me, and was there for them when they got in trouble. I had their fronts *and* their backs. Dragging their asses away from danger when they did something stupid, and as they got older, cleaning up the puke when they drank to numb the pain. When Brett needed to kick someone's ass, I fought him. When Dylan skipped school, I hauled him to classes. When Carson seemed like he was disappearing altogether, I forced him back into life." He shrugged. "And I'd do it all over again. For any one of them."

"They're lucky to have you. It's no wonder you guys are so close."

"It's a wonder we made it to being respectable adults." He smiled at the joke he and his brothers tossed around like a football.

"That's why your parents divorced?"

He nodded. "It was a blessing and a curse. I remember a time when they loved each other, but it wasn't enough. Their love turned venomous, and when I was sixteen it got worse. Not violent, but volatile. My brothers and I had this fort in the woods. Two by fours thrown together with plywood. Kid stuff. But it was *ours*. When it was raining or snowing and the fights echoed off the walls, we'd hole up in there. One night I lost it. I'd had enough of running, hiding, not having anyplace that felt like home. I left my brothers in the fort and confronted my father."

"At sixteen?" Her voice escalated with surprise.

He nodded. "I was angry, invincible, standing on the edge of a very thin line between freedom and juvy—and lucky my father didn't deck my ass. He'd always been cutthroat, but he'd turned into a miserable bastard. I'll never forget that night. It was sleeting, and we'd left without our coats. I was drenched, shaking from anger more than cold probably, but shaking nonetheless. At sixteen I was already six two or three, probably all of a hundred sixty pounds. Nothing compared to my dad, who stands six four and two thirty. But I was full of rage—at the world, at God, at my parents, myself. I told my father we'd had enough and to get the hell out of the house." His mind reeled back almost twenty years to his father's confused face, and in a flash, how the confusion had morphed to anger. He closed his eyes briefly as the verbal rage that ensued slammed into him. Refusing to give his father that power, he forced himself to continue speaking.

"I don't remember exactly what I said, but I didn't back down. My mother was crying and begging me to stop, but all I saw was Lorelei in that hospital bed, a shadow of the sister she'd been, and the funeral. The awful, terrible funeral and my brothers hiding in the woods. We'd lost our sister, and I felt like we were losing each other at breakneck speed. I think I felt like it was a choice. My dad or the family." That realization gave him pause. It was another thing he hadn't picked apart until just now. Another piece of him Amanda dug up and forced him to face with love and kindness he didn't deserve.

"Mick," she whispered, holding his hand.

He couldn't stop talking, didn't want to, until she knew it all. "He left, but he came back the next day, and things changed. Got quiet again, tense, scary in a way that it had never been. Like we were all waiting for the glass floor to shatter, only it felt like it already had and we were suspended by something tentative and dark, waiting to drop onto the shards. Then one day he moved out, and..." He didn't really remember anything specific after that until weeks later.

"One day life was easier again. Not normal. Not fine, but easier. Our father's still miserable, and our mother is warm and loving again, but empty. So damn empty."

Amanda rested her head on his shoulder. He knew she was processing all that he'd said, probably thinking less of him for breaking up his family for good. But it was out there now. His past, his present, his future, all wrapped up in one big mess, and she wasn't pushing him away.

She was there by his side, her head on his shoulder, giving him the strength to breathe.

"You were there for everyone," she said. "You took care of them. Who took care of you?"

The question pained him, because he'd always felt guilty for feeling a little bit of that back then, at a time when he needed to hold everyone else together.

"I was a man. I didn't need to be taken care of."

"Everyone needs taking care of." She rose onto her knees and straddled his lap.

"You want to fool around?" The halfhearted joke hung heavily between them. Her eyes went serious, seeing right though his smoke screen.

"I don't want you to run away."

He wrapped his arms around her, wondering if she knew he'd been running since he was a teenager and he didn't intend to stop.

"When the judge asks you something you don't like, you pace like a caged tiger," she said with a small smile. "When a client tries to back you into a corner, you put them in their place, but then you leave them alone to stew over the slaughtering you've given them and you pace the halls. And sometimes when your brothers come to see you, you leave them in your office and look like you're chewing on nails while you wear a path in the hall."

She had him pegged on all accounts. "You watch me that closely?"

A flush rose on her cheeks and she pursed her lips. "Purely for research purposes." She placed her hands on his chest and her expression softened again. "My boss taught me to listen for holes, discrepancies, anything that might shadow the truth."

He looked away, his gut fisting for a whole new reason. He didn't want her to see the effect it had on him knowing she'd been watching him so closely, but more importantly, he didn't want her to see how dark he was on the inside. How villainous the part was that he didn't confess.

"Like avoiding eye contact," she said softly. "Mick?"

She was like the moon, her gravity pulling at him, distorting his plans, his thoughts, and causing tides of anger and frustration to ebb and flow against the warmer feelings she evoked. Powerless to resist her, he met her all-knowing gaze. He gritted his teeth, struggling to mask his inner turmoil and force his thoughts into order. Or at least into deceptive calmness.

A quizzical look washed over her, and he thought he'd pulled it off, but when she pressed her hands to his cheeks and touched her forehead to his, it sparked another internal storm.

"What about you, Mick? You lost your baby sister. What was your role for her? What was hers to you?"

"Amanda." The warning was weak at best.

She lifted her head, leaving her hands on his cheeks. "You owe me nothing, and I trust that come Monday, everything we've said and done will still be our secret. But I've bared myself to you, and I'm offering you a chance to unburden your heart, Mick. With me. You're safe with me."

His mind refused to register the significance of her words. The world had always spun around him, buzzing with distractions from all the guilt he carried. He used that whirling buzz to pull him from moment to moment, day to day. Filling his head with information, pushing himself to excel in college and law school, building the practice, watching out for his brothers—they were all distractions from the guilt and pain and loneliness that threatened to drown him at every turn. Over the last few months, watching out for Amanda had become his biggest distraction of all, and he'd had to find other distractions to keep himself from thinking of her.

Accepting her offer meant facing the darkest part of his past, and facing that demon meant jumping into a dark, cavernous abyss he wasn't sure he'd survive.

Chapter Eleven

VOLATILE. EXPLOSIVE. TERRIFIED. Amanda cataloged Mick's emotions as they assailed him, one after another at a thunderous pace, pounding through his body, muscle by muscle, vein by vein, reminding her of the Incredible Hulk. He gripped her just above her ribs, hard yet restrained, and lifted her to her feet.

"Ready to hit that bar?" he asked sharply, and stepped away.

Momentarily rebuffed, she watched him retreat, then snapped out of her hurt stupor and grabbed his arm. He spun around angrily. His glare was not nearly as threatening as the pain she saw behind it.

Gutted by the look in his eyes, she didn't think, didn't speak, as she wrapped her arms around his waist and pressed her cheek to his chest. His heartbeat sprinted, as if trying to escape its confines. The rigidity of his body told her he wished he could do the same.

"Amanda," he growled coldly.

She held him tighter, knowing that doing so might

bring an end to their weekend. He'd probably pack them up and drive back to the city tonight, but it was a risk she was willing to take. He'd given her so many things. Freedom, relief, a sense of safety. Those things barely scratched the surface. He had her thinking about herself differently. Every time he told her she was being seductive when she wasn't trying brought awareness and understanding. But as she held him, she realized he'd given her something much better, much more meaningful. He'd given her a piece of himself that she didn't think he ever expected to share. If he chose to cut their weekend short, at least he'd go home with this moment, knowing there was one person he could trust.

"Amanda," he said a little warmer, though still riddled with frustration.

"You need this." Her head told her to turn and walk away, but her heart wanted no part of that plan. She tipped her face up, taking in his tight jaw, the bulging veins on his neck, and the trouble swimming in his eyes.

"You can't possibly know what I need."

His words stung, despite his soft tone.

"That's a shame, because you're a good man, and someone should." She released him, and for a minute they stared at each other. Unmoving. Unrelenting. Unable or unwilling to give in, or to sever the bond that had formed between them, and he was apparently just as unwilling to deepen it.

Everyone had their demons. It hurt knowing she'd laid her demons out before him and he didn't want to fully reciprocate. But he hadn't abused her trust. He'd treated her well, better than well. He'd made her feel special and safe. His refusal might hurt, but, she reminded herself, this unexpected discussion wasn't tied to her decision to open up to him. She fought to remember that. This wasn't a tit-for-tat weekend. This was a Sex Adventure Weekend. An agreement that had nothing to do with baring their souls, regardless of if they chose—or didn't choose—to do so.

She drew her hands behind her back, urging herself to accept their agreement for what it was—*pinchigan, pinchigan, pinchigan*. Shocking her heart into submission, she reached for his hand. "How about that drink?"

"Amanda." He sounded apologetic, but he said nothing more.

The drive back to Sweetwater was nothing like the ride up. Sounds came at her muted, then sharp. Cold air whipped against her skin. Vibrations sent disturbing quakes to her chaotic thoughts.

The bar.

Drinks.

That would do them both some good. Take the edge off. All she had to do was play it cool until then.

When they arrived at Sweetwater, they parked the motorcycle in the garage behind the house and ascended the stairs in uncomfortable silence.

Mick pushed open the door and said, "I'll get our stuff."

"We're leaving?" Panic carried her words. *Way to play it cool.*

He turned to her with disappointment in his eyes. "Do you want to leave?"

"No, but you said you're getting our stuff, and after I pushed you up on the mountain, I thought...If you want to go back, we can. You've helped me a lot, and I appreciate it. I—"

"Am rambling," he said, tugging her against him.

The possessive move sent reassurance soaring through her. *Pinchigan! Pinchigan!*

"Adorably," he added as he touched his lips to hers, settling her worries even more.

"I'm sorry I pushed," she said softly. "It wasn't any of my business."

"You did what any good friend would."

Friend. The pit of her stomach sank. *Pull up your big-girl panties.* She swallowed hard, determined to be just as good of a friend to him as he had been to her.

He slid his hand to the nape of her neck, brushing his thumb over the spot he loved to kiss and sending threads of hope through her. *We're friends.* The reminder did nothing to quell the love swelling inside her, or the hope that he might share whatever he was holding back with her after all.

"I'm not an easy man to get to know. There's a reason I don't do relationships."

If she opened her mouth to speak she'd want to reason with him, to tell him he'd feel better once he got whatever it was out of his system. But that wasn't their deal, so she kept her mouth shut and nodded.

"I thought we'd stay on my boat. Would you rather stay here?"

"No. The boat sounds lovely."

He watched her for a long, silent beat. "Okay, let's get our things."

She had to work really hard not to let disappointment get the better of her. As they gathered their things, she focused on the warm, masculine rooms they'd rushed through earlier. It seemed like days had passed since they were last there. The furniture was heavy, rustic, not elaborate or expensive like the furniture in his apartment in the city. She stopped in the doorway of the bathroom, remembering the things they'd done in the shower and how lovingly he'd washed her afterward. A rush of emotions swelled in her chest. She tried desperately to keep them at bay as she gathered her toiletries. Mick was in the other room, but his presence and masculine scent was inescapable. She closed her eyes and breathed him in. She felt a deep connection to him, and when they were on the mountain, she thought he'd begun to feel the same. But maybe she had read too much into his confession and the way he was treating her. Either way, she had no regrets about their time together, beyond the notion that she'd probably have to give up her job.

"About ready?"

She startled. Mick stood in the doorway, his leather bag hung from one hand, and his face—*God, she loved his face*—was unreadable. So she'd been wrong about the connection. Okay, as much as that hurt, she could deal with it, because as much as this weekend was shaking her up like a snow globe, it was also satiating a place inside her she'd reserved just for Mick.

"I'm ready." She reached for her bag, and Mick's hand covered hers.

"Men like to feel needed, and it's past sunset. You're in seduction mode, remember?"

Right, the deal. She was supposed to be picking him up at the bar, not just easing her nerves with alcohol. She'd need many more drinks to soothe the butterflies and bees warring inside her.

She followed him down to the car. "About tonight," she said as he put the bags in the trunk. "You've done a great job of cluing me in to things, so maybe we should forgo the seduction tonight."

He opened the passenger door without responding. She slid into the seat and tried to read his body language as he rounded the car and climbed in behind the wheel, but even with his brooding, all that registered was how much she wanted to be near him.

He settled into the car and drove around the lake. "Not feeling up to the challenge?"

"I thought you might not be into it, after everything that happened earlier." She peered out the window at the cobblestone streets and the shops lining them on the way down to the marina. Old-fashioned awnings shaded big picture windows, and above each shop was a balcony, like Mick's house, which had the bookstore below. She wondered about that house, and the store, but now wasn't the time to ask, so she focused on the lights of the marina shimmering against the night sky.

"I'm into you, Amanda," he said out of the blue. "Don't ever doubt that."

She turned, confused and shocked. She'd hoped to get a read on his expression, since he'd spoken so matter-of-factly, but if there had been any change, she'd missed it. He was staring absently at the road.

She made small talk to try to ease her nerves. "How does this work? Do we walk in together but pretend we're strangers?"

He parked at the far end of the marina and took her hand in his. "See the pub on the other side of the boat house?"

She spotted Dutch's Pub anchoring a row of shops. "Yes."

"We'll get ready, and then I'll walk you over. You'll

go in first, and a little while later I'll show up." He rubbed the spot between her thumb and index finger, then pressed a kiss there. "The rest is up to you."

If it were up to her, they'd skip the seduction and go straight to the part where he ravaged her, murmuring sexy things that made her forget how to think, and then they'd hit repeat for the rest of their lives.

She was getting more nervous just thinking about sitting in the bar waiting for him. She needed an edge, like Mick had when he was in the courtroom. Something that would make him want to study her. She mentally skimmed *The Handbook. The Perfect Entrance, Chapter Twenty-One.*

Oh yeah, she could do this.

Maybe.

I hope.

"I have a better idea," she offered. "How far is your boat?"

He stepped from the car and came around to help her out. "Let me get the bags and I'll show you." After retrieving the bags from the trunk, they walked past the docks and around an outcropping of trees, and another dock came into view. At the far end was a single slip, and there, basking in the moonlight, was a gorgeous yacht. Aqua lights dove like darts from the bottom of the vessel into the inky water. White lights twinkled around the perimeter of the decks, giving the beautiful yacht a magical appearance that took Amanda's breath away.

Yacht? She touched Mick's forearm, wondering what other things in his life he'd minimized and why. "I think we need to have a talk about semantics."

**

HARLEY DUTCH SLID another drink across the bar, skeptically eyeing Mick. "It's not like you to watch the door."

Mick watched Dutch wipe down the bar, thinking the same damn thing. It had been a long time since he'd been on an actual date, not that this was a date, but it had the hallmarks of one. After he'd showered, he'd taken far too long deciding what to wear. His typical weekend attire was jeans and a comfortable T-shirt, but tonight felt different, and he wasn't all that sure that it only had to do with being seduced by Amanda. The thought that he might have competition had irritatingly played in his mind as he'd picked out his slacks and white button-down. He'd hated the idea of her walking alone from the boat to the bar, despite the safe town, but she'd been adamant about him going first. He'd been sitting in the bar for forty-five minutes, his gut churning as each of those minutes passed, wondering what was going through her mind and if his confession had changed her view of him for the worse.

He lifted his glass to Harley with a nod and took a drink. "One of those nights, I guess." He purposely gave nothing away about his and Amanda's seductive game. He didn't want to embarrass Amanda, and even though it was a bitch to think about, he didn't want to embarrass himself, either. He'd checked out the other guys in the bar, all of whom had an air of attraction he didn't—a clean conscience.

"Right." Harley elongated the word and shook his head. "There's nothing I haven't heard, seen, or wished I could unsee." His lips quirked up in a knowing grin that reached his deep-set blue eyes. Harley was Mick's age, burly as a grizzly, with a shock of brown hair to match. He was a good-looking, smart guy, and a hell of a nice one at that. He'd given up a thriving finance career in the city to return home when his father had taken ill. That was three years ago. He'd taken over his father's pub and had never looked back.

Competition.

Mick gulped down that thought with his drink, wondering what the hell was wrong with him. It wasn't like Amanda was going to come into the bar looking to seduce someone else. Although he had been a bit of a dick when they were on the overlook. His mind reeled back to the night of the bar crawl. They'd connected across the floor immediately, with an intensity that drew him like a tiger to fresh meat. But she'd approached other men instead of approaching him. He stared into his drink, swirling the amber liquid as he picked that uncomfortable fact apart.

A sandy-haired guy slid onto a barstool to Mick's left, leaving one empty seat between them. "How's it going?"

"Not bad," Mick said, reluctantly cataloging the guy's deeply tanned, chiseled features and sharp green eyes. He had to stop this. He was acting like a jealous punk.

Harley handed the guy a Guinness. "Greer, this is Mick. Mick's up from the city, too. Greer's a movie producer," he said to Mick. The almost indiscernible shake of his head told Mick that Harley didn't like the guy. "He's in town to see his family."

Greer took a swig of his beer. "Ah. Nothing better than ice-cold beer. What do you do, Mick?"

"I tinker with the law," Mick said. He spent the

next few minutes listening to Greer talk about himself. His office was a few blocks from Mick's. He dropped names like he was tossing seed to birds and blew so much hot air it was a wonder he wasn't floating against the ceiling. Mick downed another drink, catching an eye roll and a chuckle from Harley.

Harley fixed him another drink, which he was more than thankful for.

"Mind if I sit here?" The underlying shyness in Amanda's voice made Mick's gut go ten types of crazy.

He and Greer both turned and drank in every inch of her luscious curves in a hip-hugging, thigh-baring little black number with long sleeves and a sexy lace-up thing going on from collarbone to the sweet depths of her cleavage. *Holy hell*. His cock twitched at the black leather spike-heeled boots running up her long legs and over her knees. Next to her, Greer was practically salivating. *Asshole*.

"Absolutely," Greer said in a hungry voice that made Mick want to punch him in the face.

Amanda sat on the seat between them, turning her attention to Greer, which kicked Mick out of his lust-driven stupor and back into the game.

"Thank you," she purred, wiggling her ass so her shoulders rubbed them both.

"Harley," Mick said in the least annoyed voice he could manage, which still came out a bit pissed. "Get the lady a sidecar?"

Harley smirked. "Coming right up."

Amanda glanced at Mick, blinking lengthened lashes and smoky eyes. Her full lips were painted fire-engine red, glistening as if she'd just licked them. He was pretty sure she had, given that it was one of her nervous habits he'd noticed—and adored. Her normally straight hair framed her face and cascaded to her shoulders in gentle waves. He wanted to tangle his hands in her hair and kiss that seductive paint off her lips.

"How did you know that was a favorite of mine?" she asked with an air of anonymity that was beyond impressive.

The same way I know you like coffee with one sugar and two creams, and romance, and the way I know that when I touch those freckles on your neck, you shiver all over. Because I pay attention. Because I care. It was torture, fighting the urge to claim her with a possessive hand at the base of her spine or on her exposed, tempting thigh. But he'd made a deal, and he took his deals very seriously.

He lifted his drink to his lips and shifted his attention to the bottles on the shelf behind the bar, then said, "Lucky guess."

Tossing back his drink in one gulp, he held the empty glass up toward Harley, who looked confused. Mick was right there with him. What the hell was he doing? He felt Amanda's eyes burning into him. No doubt he'd left her a little flustered, but he wasn't about to check, because she could do this. She could nail it, and she needed to know that.

"I like a man who knows what women want," she said confidently.

He turned, catching Greer's challenging gaze over her shoulder.

"Then look this way, sweetheart," Greer said—*and she did.* "Shoes, Chanel bags, fast cars, candlelit dinners, and a rich man on her arm."

She lifted her glass, her gorgeous eyes moving between Greer and Mick, then settled on Greer, tweaking every one of Mick's nerves.

"That's *so* much better than a guess." She leaned closer to the *wrong* man.

Mick caught the silent message in Greer's snide grin loud and clear—*Dibs*.

Dibs, my ass. Mick Bad backed down to no one.

Amanda glanced at Mick again, amusement playing in her expression. A few whispered sentences would have her climbing in his lap, but he'd given her this night as her own and had promised to critique her efforts. Fuck him for being an idiot, but a deal was a deal.

"Are you from this sweet little town?" she asked Greer.

The asshole scoffed. "I live in Manhattan. I'm just taking a few days to chill." And off he went on a diatribe about his production company, the stars he'd worked with, and his self-inflated importance. He ordered Amanda another drink and made jokes that she pretended to laugh at.

Mick was surprised he knew the difference between her fake and real laughter, but nothing about Amanda went under his radar anymore. Her finger was grooving along the side of her glass, which meant she was very bored and a little nervous. She sat up straighter, arching her back just enough to make her breasts press against the lace, and crossed her legs, while shifting her eyes to the wall behind the bar. A perfectly executed seductive move. Her skimpy dress inched up even higher, drawing Mick's *and* Greer's attention and causing a five-alarm temperature spike. *One sentence. That's all it would take. Hell, one word, said in the right tone, with the right smile, and she was his.*

"I didn't catch your name. I'm Greer." The asshole flashed a smile that Mick was sure would make many women melt—until he opened his big mouth.

Amanda held out a hand, bent at the wrist. "Dita. Dita Vandercross."

Greer took the invitation and kissed the back of her hand. It took every ounce of Mick's restraint not to tear the guy's lips right off his face.

Amanda angled her body toward Mick, studying him the way she sometimes did when they met with clients. Reading him. He wondered if she saw the way she made him hot and weak at once, or if it was muddied by the visceral need to kick Greer out of the pub. Her eyes were on the move, traveling over his features, lingering on his lips long enough for his mouth to water. Her lips curved up in a wicked smile, and she continued eye-fucking her way down his body, painfully slowly, like lava burning him from the outside in. When she reached his lap, she licked her lips again, definitely not nervously. His cock remembered the feel of those luscious lips around him, the heat of her mouth as she sucked him off, and he ached for a replay. He gripped his glass to keep from grabbing her and waited out every breath-sucking second as she raked his body over the coals again, visually feasting on him on the way back up before finally meeting his heated gaze.

"And you are?" A pensive shimmer appeared in the shadow of her eyes.

He couldn't help but gloat, tossing Greer a watch-how-it's-done smirk.

"*Bad*," he promised. "Mick Bad."

Chapter Twelve

AMANDA SWALLOWED TIGHTLY against the pulse swelling at the base of her throat, as if her heart had risen from her chest for all to see. She thought she could play this game, seduce another man in hopes of raising jealousy in Mick. But Mick's presence was like a drug, lulling her in. He wasn't just looking at her. He was devouring her, sending sinful promises, driving them deeper with every breath, until she could feel every last one of them. She tried to deny the knot forming in her stomach, to write it off as nerves, but there was no mistaking the damp heat between her legs.

"That sounds like a promise," she finally managed. "Or is it just another hopeful guess?"

Greer coughed to cover a laugh.

Mick didn't flinch as he leaned closer, holding her captive with his piercing stare, and said, "A *hopeful* guess is that you aren't wearing anything beneath that dress. A *lucky* guess is knowing I'm going to get lucky tonight and guessing you haven't realized it yet." He slid a hand to the nape of her neck, alighting prickles of heat beneath her skin, holding her so close she could smell the alcohol on his breath. "And I *always* make good on my promises."

He leaned back, giving rise to cooler air that whisked over her skin. He turned his attention to the television in the far corner behind the bar, sipping his drink as if he hadn't just made her cave in on herself.

Greer ordered her another drink and pressed his leg against hers. "I was out in LA schmoozing with Spielberg, and..."

If she had to listen to one more word about who this guy knew, she was going to scream. Her plan was obviously not working. She'd thought she had Mick, but he was staring off at the television and this guy was so into himself he didn't need an audience. She stepped off the stool. Mick turned. Greer continued talking to himself.

"I'm going to the—"

"Mick!" A petite blonde practically leaped over a table and threw her arms around Mick's neck.

He embraced her for a long moment. Very long. The type of long that said he missed her, too.

"Piper. You look gorgeous. How are you?" He motioned to the stool on his other side, and Piper slid her perfect size-two ass onto it like she owned it as Mick shot a smile at Harley. "Harley, Disaronno on the rocks, please."

"Little girls' room," Amanda mumbled to herself. She grabbed her purse and stalked off. Thankfully, she had the bathroom to herself to fume, and maybe to pout. She wanted to pace, but the heels of her boots were like walking on toothpicks. And if that wasn't enough, the leather wasn't tight enough, so she was constantly pulling them up. She'd walked halfway to the bar hunched over and clinging to the top edge of the boots so they wouldn't shimmy down her calves and gather around her ankles. With pacing off the table, she had no choice but to stand and stare at herself in the stupid mirror, thinking of Mick hugging Piper. What kind of name was that? Was she an instrument?

Had he *played* her?

Oh God. Not helpful.

She couldn't believe Mick didn't even introduce her! That was just plain rude. And that little blonde? All perky and perfect in her snug white V-neck and boyfriend jeans that hugged her skinny freaking hips. Amanda couldn't get one rounded hip into the entirety of them.

She tugged open her purse and eyed *The Handbook*. She'd followed the rules all the way down to waxing body parts that should never feel such pain. *I can pull dark secrets from witnesses, but give me one man to seduce, and without a wig I'm a total failure.* Well, fuck that. She was *not* going to fail. There were plenty of men in this bar, and she'd seduce every one of them until she had it down pat. *Then* she'd get the only one she wanted.

She took another glance at the woman in the mirror and was surprised to see she was smoking hot, and not a woman but a *babe*. The pit of her stomach twisted, and she pointed at the unfamiliar vixen.

"Shut up. Just shut up."

"Blond," she said with distaste. "Ha! I was blond for two nights, and I know damn well brunettes have more fun." She hoisted her purse over her shoulder, determined to hook at least three—*two; two sounds doable*—men before the night was over. *One. Okay, one man. No, two. One for practice, and Mick.*

She pushed the door open and bent to tug up her damn boots.

"That's the perfect height for that pretty mouth of yours."

Motherfucker. She straightened her back, meeting Greer's revolting glare. She had seductive powers, all right; she just had very bad aim. She'd gotten the wrong guy...*again.*

He stepped forward, and she retreated—right into the wall.

"Sweetheart," he said, pressing into her. "Do you have any idea how lucky you are to have landed next to *me* tonight?"

"Yeah, that's exactly what I was thinking." Sarcasm dripped from every word. She tried to maneuver around him, but he trapped her with his arm. She rolled her eyes, annoyed with the guy for blocking her when she was feeling so confident.

"How about we go someplace private?"

She needed some type of loser radar. Why wasn't *that* in the flippin' handbook? "I don't think so," she said, debating a swift knee to his privates.

Mick came around the corner and stopped at the end of the hall. In a blink he took in the scene, anger turned to amusement. He arched a brow, shaking his head, his message clear. *What have you gotten yourself into this time?*

She clenched her jaw, giving him an *I've got this* look. Or at least she hoped she did, though she had no idea if she had this or not.

Mick slid his hand into his pocket and leaned his

shoulder against the wall. His casual stance didn't mask the instant his eyes went from amused to lethal. She read that message perfectly clearly, too. *Take care of it, or I will.*

"If you don't mind," Amanda said firmly to the jerk in front of her. "I'd like to return to the bar."

Greer, apparently oblivious to Mick's presence, took her wrist and pinned it to the wall. "Oh, I mind, all right. Do you have any idea *who* I am? I could have any woman, any actress—"

Mick's hand landed heavily on Greer's shoulder, startling both of them. Without a word, he kicked the men's room door open and smiled at Amanda as he threw Greer into the restroom. "I'll be right back, Ms. Vandercross."

Amanda's hand flew to her heart. She was more annoyed than scared of Mr. Hot Air, but the brawling noises coming from the bathroom had her tipping to the scared side. She would have kneed the asshole if she'd had to. Damn it. This was the second time Mick had intervened on her behalf, and as hot as it was to see him in alpha mode—and it was smokin' hot—she wasn't a frigging damsel in distress.

Mick came out of the bathroom a few minutes later smoothing his shirt over his chest. He stretched his neck to the right, then to the left, and put an arm around Amanda's waist. She glanced over their shoulders, wondering what he'd done to Greer.

"Maybe we went too fast," he said, leading her out of the hallway. "Maybe you need the remedial course."

"What does that mean? I could have gotten him off."

Mick cocked a brow. "That's what I was worried about."

171

She couldn't help but laugh.

"You were gone so long I thought you'd fallen in the toilet. I guess being pinned by Andrew Dice Clay isn't much better." He shook his head. "You're *too* good at seduction. I was ready to kick the guy's ass when you offered him your hand."

"Really?" Elation sent her up on her toes for a kiss, and her heel slid out from under her, sending her down, down, down. Her hands flailed toward the ceiling. She clenched her jaw, preparing for the impact—but her crazy mind screamed *I did it! I seduced you!* She landed with a jolt, gasping for air and smiling, stuck in some ridiculously happy place. She was lying flat on her back, a dozen pairs of eyes gaping at her from above. And beside her, Mick was on his knees, returning her insane smile, his arms outstretched beneath her, and he was giving her that look again—*What have you gotten yourself into this time?*

"I did it," she said foolishly.

He lifted her to her feet and righted her dress, giving her thighs a titillating squeeze in the process. "Baby," he said, smooth as butter and rich as silk. "I never stood a chance."

How he understood her cryptic message was beyond her. Wait, no, it wasn't. This was Mick, and whether he liked it or not, he *got* her. *You're my one. I knew it all along.*

Greer stumbled past, grumbling under his breath. His hair and shoulders were dripping wet as he headed out the door.

She looked up at Mick. "What did you—"

"Not nearly enough." He pulled her in close, and she gladly went. "Now that you've successfully seduced two men, how about we get out of here? There are way too many guys visually gobbling you up, and with your penchant for going pantiless, I imagine you gave them an eyeful of your goodies when you went down."

**

AMANDA CLUNG TO Mick as they left the bar, undoubtedly so she wouldn't fall off her fuck-me heels again.

"Wait!" She stopped at the edge of the parking lot and set her hands on her hips. "I can't do this anymore."

Shit, was this the other shoe falling? She realized she could seduce a man just fine and didn't need him and his fucking past hanging around?

She plopped down on her butt and lifted one leg. "Please pull these suckers off. I swear, if you help me out of these torture traps, I'll do anything you want."

Mick chuckled and took her heel in his hand, trying to avert his eyes from the nakedness between her legs, but it was too damn tempting. He'd surely paved his way straight to hell already. Why not ensure the trip? He followed her legs to the sweetness between them.

"Hey!" Amanda snapped her fingers and waved them in front of her face. "Eyes up here, mister."

"When did you get so pushy? I'm kind of digging it." He tugged her boot off.

"*You* are a god." Amanda fell back, arms stretched out to her sides on the pavement, and let out a loud sigh.

Damn, he did *love* her laugh. "A god, huh?"

She lifted her other leg, and Mick grabbed hold. He knew she wasn't drunk, but she seemed looser and more relaxed than she had in, he realized, *weeks*.

She pushed up on her palms and jauntily cocked her head to the side. "I don't know. Now I can't really tell. Maybe after you take that boot off, I'll see your godliness again."

He pulled the boot off, draped both over his shoulder, and helped her to her feet. "Let's go to the boat and see how the view of my godliness looks from there."

"Yacht," she corrected him.

He put his arm around her, acutely aware of the late hour and their time together dwindling. "You have a thing about semantics. Tell me about this godliness I possess."

"Not until you admit it's a yacht." She laughed, and it struck him straight in the center of his heart.

"Okay, it's a small yacht. Who cares?" They walked around the trees toward the dock. "Now, back to my godliness."

"Like you need an ego boost? Maybe you should go back into the bar and find that pretty little blonde again."

A smile tugged at his lips. "Ms. Vandercross, is that jealousy I hear?" *Because I like it a hell of a lot more than I should.*

"No!" She pushed from his side as they stepped onto the dock. "It was just an observation."

"Hm. Interesting. None of my other staff members has ever made such an observation."

"So," she said softly, "you've gone out with other girls from the office?"

He pulled her away from the edge of the dock.

"Careful."

She gazed up with the doe eyes that had first captivated him. Keeping his emotions in check was getting harder by the minute.

"It's okay. You don't have to answer." She began walking toward the boat again.

"Amanda, I haven't gone out with anyone else in the office. You should know that. Have you ever seen me even flirt with any of our employees?"

She glanced at him as they made their way down the dock. "Well, no, but..."

"Careful of that green-eyed monster," he warned. "She'll make you see things that aren't there." Her brow knitted. "And the girl in the bar was Piper Dalton. She's Willow and Bridgette's sister. They have another sister and a brother, but I don't expect to see either this trip. Piper is a builder and incredibly good with boats. She takes care of my place and boat while I'm out of town. I called her when we stopped for gas and asked her to stock the boat with food, drinks, set the timers for the lights. That's all. She's a friend." He helped her aboard and kept hold of her hand.

"That was nice of her," she said with a sweet smile. "And of you, actually, to think ahead like that. Thank you. I'm sorry if I sounded weird, I just..." She shook her head. "I guess it's just a weird night."

"It's been a nice night, and an intense couple of days." He was having trouble believing that's all it had been. "Let's take the boat out and anchor away from the shore for the night. Then we'll talk."

Chapter Thirteen

TWO HOURS LATER Mick and Amanda lay on a bed of blankets and pillows on the deck of the yacht, gazing up at the stars. Neither was hungry for a meal, so they had cheese and crackers and shared a bottle of wine. A chilly breeze swept off the lake, but Amanda felt toasty warm. That could have been from the wine, but she had a feeling it had more to do with the man beside her.

"Tell me about your bookstore. I'd imagine you could have bought any house you wanted. Why that one? Why not a cabin in the woods?" She propped herself up on her elbow, struck by how peaceful Mick appeared in the moonlight. His hair fell away from his face, and for the first time since they'd come together, there was no tension in his forehead or in the muscles around his jaw. She wrenched herself away from her ridiculous preoccupation with his face and lay on her back. She had the darn thing memorized. *My fantasy man.* He was etched into the recesses of her mind forever.

"I don't know much about it."

She looked at him, and he smiled. "You said you owned it."

"I do, but you probably noticed it's closed." He propped up on an elbow as she had earlier. "I didn't want a remote cabin. I like the small town, the people here, the camaraderie. When I was looking for a house, I met a woman named Flossie McBride. She's a tiny thing, maybe four foot ten or so, in her seventies. She and her husband, Jed, had run the bookstore for forty years, and they lived upstairs. Jed suffered a stroke and he was moved to a rehab facility on Long Island. She had to sell the house and the store to make enough money for his care." He lifted a shoulder in a casual shrug. "So I bought it and told her if she was ever ready to come back, the store would be here waiting for her."

"Aw, Mick. That's just about the sweetest thing I've ever heard. How long ago was that?"

"Four years." His gaze turned solemn. "Thankfully, Jed's still hanging on, though he needs round-the-clock care."

"I'm sorry to hear that. Four years is a long time. Do you have someone else running the store?"

"From time to time. Her granddaughter, Aurelia, comes into town every four or five weeks and opens it for a few days, does whatever Flossie advises, then leaves again. I have no need for the downstairs, and I made a promise. I always try to keep my promises."

She rolled onto her side, mirroring his position. "You are a very good man, Mr. Bad. You made me a promise, too. You were supposed to critique me tonight. How did I do? Besides the whole falling-on-my-ass thing."

"That was one of my favorite parts."

She swatted him. "Come on, be serious. It was scary going into the bar and pretending to be someone else."

"Why? Isn't that what you did at the bar crawl?"

His face grew serious, his eyes tender, and everything around them seemed to still and quiet, as if the world were waiting for her answer. He reached over and took her hand, squeezing it gently, and she knew he really cared, even if he didn't want to admit it. She held on to that thought gently, as if the wrong move might scare it away. She ached to tell him the truth. *It was scary because I was seducing you, and as much as it was a game and this was only a weekend, I can't escape the feeling that it's so much more. I don't want to escape it.*

But that confession would surely break the moment into a million unfixable pieces.

"Yes, but it was easier with the wig and makeup. I think it must be easier for guys to put themselves out there like that than it is for women. For women, it's strange. Or maybe that's just me, which it probably is, because I know Ally was able to do it and never felt like I did tonight or the night of the bar crawl, which honestly wasn't easier. It's all scary. Acting like I wanted to be in control, when every ounce of my being really just wants to feel wanted and loved"—*for who I am, not for who I can be for a few hours*—"was scary."

Silence fell around them again, heavy, hot, and chilling at once, as if her confession consumed them. He watched her steadily, but behind the tenderness another emotion brewed. Guilt? Fear? Anger? She couldn't be sure, but neither was good. Did he regret this weekend? Had she gotten too close?

"You could have fooled me," he said evenly. Not cold, not warm. He just put it out there. "You were cool and confident."

"Come on." She tried to lighten the air with a feigned laugh. "You promised to critique me, so lay it on me. Give it to me straight."

He continued staring with that strange mix of emotions. Her belly fluttered and tightened in response.

"You could act colder," he said. "Maybe even bitchier. Like you don't really care if you're going to hook up with the guy or not."

"Hard to get. People want what they can't have. I can see the benefit." Was that what he was doing? Throwing off I-want-you and I-won't-go-there vibes to make her want him even more? Or was that just her absurdly hopeful heart creating a mirage again?

"And don't laugh at stupid jokes." He cracked a smile. "Let the asshole know he's not funny."

"Why? Isn't that the whole point? To build the guy up?" She lay back again and stared up at the stars. "There are way more rules than I thought."

He ran his finger lightly down the length of her arm. It was a tender, thoughtful, and seductive touch, and it surprised her given the intense look in his eyes. "And wear underwear, for Christ's sake."

She turned and glared. "You loved knowing I wasn't wearing underwear."

"Exactly."

"I don't get it."

"I liked knowing it, because you were there to seduce me, but I hated knowing it when you were talking to Greer."

She turned her face to the sky, hoping he couldn't see the smile she had no hopes of holding back. Knowing he was jealous made her giddy.

"Seems like it worked, then. I'm definitely going to continue not wearing underwear when I'm in seduction mode. What else?" She didn't have to look to know his face had grown tight. Tension sparked from his body, heating the air between them and bringing her even more satisfaction.

"No hooker boots," he said sharply.

Definitely wearing hooker boots from now on. She heard him breathing harder and imagined his eyes narrow and angry. *Maybe even to work.* "What else?"

"You could go easier on the makeup."

Smoky eyes. Check. "Really?" This was too much fun. He sounded like a shaken-up soda bottle, ready to *pop*!

"Yes. Don't try so damn hard."

She fed off of his attraction, drawing courage she didn't know she possessed, and turned toward him. His expression was thunderous.

"You shouldn't do this." It was a command as clear and dark as his jealous stare.

"This, as in critique, or this as in, play any more games this weekend?" Swallowing the fear that leaped into her throat, she steeled herself for an answer that would surely tear her to shreds.

"Don't do it anymore, Amanda. It's a mistake." He spoke quietly, calmly, despite the tumultuous vibes he was emitting.

She was still unsure if he meant the weekend or seducing men in general. Tormented by confusing emotions, she tried to catch her breath. He shifted beside her, and she closed her eyes, telling herself to take a step back. This was a game, this fucked-up weekend of theirs, and she couldn't change the rules midstream no matter how badly she wanted to. She felt him move away. Cooler air washed along her body, driving the hurt deeper. She squeezed her eyes tighter to ward off the unwanted ache of losing what she never had and struggled to erect a wall of defense against her attraction to him. In the next breath he was coming down over her, his thighs pressed to hers, his big hands cradling her head. She was struck by his tormented gaze and confused by her desire to ease his torment and soothe her own, rendering thoughts and actions equally impossible.

**

THE KNOT IN Mick's gut loosened as he came down over Amanda, easing the gnawing, burning anger and jealousy that had nearly overpowered him. He needed this. He needed *her*. But she didn't go soft beneath him as she had before. She was rigid, her mouth pressed into a tight line, knotting his insides again. The long, deep looks they exchanged fed the fear and panic as completely as they fed his lust and affection. He could fix this, make her *his,* and calm the tsunami that swamped him. But stepping through that door, truly opening his heart to her, would inevitably end in something dark and torturous for them both.

"Don't do it anymore, Amanda." The familiar command in his voice was weakened by the undercurrent of a spine-chilling, unfamiliar plea. He knew he needed to break their spellbinding connection, but he was incapable of walking away.

Her eyes narrowed, holding him captive with

renewed confidence. "Why?"

"Because it's dangerous. Didn't you learn that tonight?"

"I'll be careful."

She touched his biceps, offering a hint of the affection he craved *only* from her.

"You have no idea what you're getting into." He wasn't sure if he was warning her away from him, from seducing other men—or if he was warning himself not to free the emotions clawing for release.

Her fingers trailed up and down his arm, softening his resolve. "Tell me," she coaxed. "Tell me what I'm getting into."

"Amanda." The need in his voice sent a wave of apprehension through him. He'd never *needed* anyone. He was the person others needed. He was the one who sat in the hallway late at night, listening to his parents fight, standing guard in front of his brothers' doors.

"Clue me in, Mick. Give me the cold, hard facts."

He was the one Lorelei needed. *You'll never let anything happen to me, right, Mickey?*

"You know I can handle it," she urged.

He knew she could handle just about anything, but not this. No one could handle the shit storm of guilt or the general fuckedupness he carried.

"Just tell me you won't seduce strangers," he finally said. "Don't let guys *take* from you."

Her brows knitted and her eyes warmed, tugging at his heartstrings, working those knots as effectively as the ones in his gut.

"Give me a reason not to." The challenge was clear, despite the sweetness of her tone.

Tug, tug. There went another knot. Painless. Addicting. He leaned forward and pressed his lips to hers. "You know I want you."

"I don't care if you want to fuck me. I want you to want all of me."

I do want all of you. Every last ounce of you. He grazed his lips over hers, inhaling her sweet scent, filling himself with her essence. He brushed his thumb over the freckles behind her ear, knowing the effect it had on her.

"Don't think like that, baby. I can want you, but we'll never be more than what we are right here, right now."

She closed her eyes, and he pressed his lips to hers again, deepening the kiss as she rose off the blanket beneath him. Christ, he loved kissing her. She made him feel so deeply, he almost believed he could pull this off. He could have forever with Amanda. They could beat the overwhelming odds and dodge the shit storms of life. Their hips ground together in a frantic beat of want and need, and somewhere deep inside him, just out of reach, he felt a thread of hope.

She tightened her grip on his arms—and abruptly pulled away. "You're *taking*!" She pushed at his chest. "Get up. Please."

"Amanda—"

"No. I can't. Get up, Mick. Now." Fury and hurt filled her voice, blazed in her features.

He pushed to his feet and paced. "What the fuck, Amanda? What do you want from me?"

"Nothing." She looked out at the water, her arms folded over her middle. Her shoulders rose and fell to the cadence of her harsh emotions. When she turned around, looking lost and hurt, it stole his breath. "*Everything*, Mick. I want what I can't have, and I knew that before we came here."

"I can't be who you want me to be, and I've been nothing but honest about that."

"No shit. You think I'm not beating myself up over this? Wanting a man who'll never want me the same way?"

He closed the distance between them, angry with himself for getting into this position, for loving a woman he had no business—*loving. Holy hell. I love you.* He stopped in his tracks as the words swam in his head.

"Just tell me one thing." She blinked several times against damp eyes. "*Why*, Mick? Why can't you be in a relationship? I'll quit the firm, if you're worried about—"

"It's not work. There's nothing in the operating agreement about that."

"So it's me." She swallowed hard, drawing her shoulders back as she inhaled a deep breath, the way she did before entering a room to speak with a witness. She was erecting her walls. Gathering courage. The courage to accept her assumption. To accept a lie.

Not on my watch.

"It's not you, Amanda. It's never been you. It's me. I'm fucked up beyond repair. It's who I am. Who I'll always be."

She closed the remaining distance between them and slid her finger into the waist of his slacks, looking up with wide, sharp eyes. "Why? You were there for everyone when you were just a kid yourself." Her voice escalated angrily. "You protected everyone and stood up to your father, which takes bigger balls than anything else in my book. You're stronger than any other man I've ever met in every way, but relationships scare the hell out of you?" She paused, shaking her head and looking at him like he was a goddamn puzzle. "It makes no sense, Counselor. I obviously don't have all the facts."

He turned away, pacing again and scrubbing his hand down his face, grasping for control.

"What is it? Just tell me already!"

Stretched to his limit, frustrated with himself, his past, his father, this fucking world, he spun around and stalked toward her. "What do you want to hear, Amanda? That I spent years being the protective older brother? That I did it so fucking well, before my baby sister went to bed every night, I pinky swore to always protect her? Or maybe that's not enough for you. You need it *all*, right? All the gritty details? Because you're so damn good at your job, you carry it over to your personal life? Because it's not enough to trust me when I tell you that I can't do this? You want my dirty fucking secret?"

He stood so close, her heartbeat pulsed in the air between them. Tears slid down her cheeks, each one slicing him open anew. Despite the hurt, despite the accusations and misdirected guilt she didn't deserve, he couldn't stop from releasing the ghost that possessed his soul.

"When my baby sister lay in a goddamn hospital bed, frail, barely breathing, her body riddled with rashes and blisters from the poison they'd pumped through her to try to kill a villain too strong to slay." His body shook and sweat dripped from his forehead as he relived the nightmare that had long ago claimed every crevice of his being. "When she looked into my eyes and said, 'You'll never let anything happen to me, right, Mickey?' in a whisper so faint I had to strain to hear it"—he turned his face down to his trembling hands, remembering the feel of her skin, the trust she'd bestowed upon him—"I took her cheeks in my hands and I lied. I lied so fucking well, she smiled and closed her eyes. I thought she'd gone to sleep, and I begged. I fucking *pleaded* with God. *Take me. Just take me.* But God, like everything else in this fucked-up world, *isn't real.* He's a fantasy, a farce, just like the movie love you're searching for. He stole that sweet little girl, and she went *believing* in *me.* Believing a lie I had no right to tell."

Amanda reached up and brushed her fingers over his cheeks, wiping tears he didn't know had fallen. *Christ.* He'd totally lost his mind.

"You were protecting her. You wanted her to feel safe."

She stepped closer and he stepped back, holding up his palm to ward her off.

"Don't, baby. Don't make this mistake, because I'm just fucked up enough to let you."

She stepped closer again. "What mistake is that? Letting you know I care? Or believing you've carried guilt for something your teenage mind made into something it wasn't?"

He shook his head. "Don't you think I know that, Amanda? I'm not a child, and you know I'm not a stupid man. I get that the guilt that strangles me is warped and childish and twisted from the despair of losing my sister."

"Then what mistake are you referencing?"

"This fantasy you have of relationships and happily ever afters. I'm not some knight in shining armor. I've never been that guy, and I will never be that guy."

"Because of the guilt," she said flatly.

"Because I'm a realist, and that fantasy doesn't exist. Why do you think I became an attorney? Because I can expose the facts and weed out the bullshit, and every day I get to prove the value of the truth. Forever is a fantasy. Look at Bridgette and Louie. She loved so hard she gave up everything for her husband. She ran away against her family's wishes and *bam*! One car accident later, she's a single mother wondering how she'll make it from day to day with a hole in her heart that will never repair itself. Thank God she has a loving family who was there for her despite her disregard for their wishes."

She crossed shaking arms over her chest, challenging him anew. "Do you really think she would have been better off without having loved him? Without knowing what it feels like to be loved so deeply you want to throw the rest of your life away just to experience it? Do you think she'd have been better off without Louie?"

He paced again, and she grabbed his arm, holding him still and drawing anger she didn't deserve. "How the hell should I know? Would my parents have been better off if they'd never married? Hadn't lost a daughter? Hadn't lost each other?"

"So, what, then? You're scared because nothing lasts forever?"

"I'm not *scared* of anything. Don't you get that? I wish I were. How easy would it be to rush into a relationship for comfort or solace or courage or whatever other bandages can assuage fear? It's way bigger than scared, baby, and not nearly as simple."

"I just don't understand." Her shoulders slumped. "If you're not scared and it's not me, what's left?"

His heart unraveled at the defeat in her voice. Gathering her against him, he tipped her chin up and felt himself falling faster, harder, and most surprising of all, falling heart first, into her. "You make me feel like the fantasy is possible."

"Then why fight it?"

"I've been asking myself that since I realized it was you at the bar. Why fight it? I've been attracted to you for so long, it's like you're part of me. Listening to your stories about boring dates, tortured by your intellectual prowess—which, by the way, is a million times more seductive than any clothes or tactics you can buy or learn."

She smiled, and it made him ache even more. "I'm going to revisit that answer when I'm not so confused and angry and hurt, so don't think you can lay all those amazing things out there without me picking them apart, Mr. Bad. But I can't revel in the words I've waited years to hear when the look in your eyes tells me that even if you feel those things, you're not willing to stand behind them. So for now, please tell me why you're fighting it."

She clung to him, and for a long moment he let her question hang between them, because when he answered, she would never touch him again.

He lifted her hand to his lips and pressed a kiss to the freckles that had initially led them to this moment. Then he slid his hand to the nape of her neck and lifted her hair, revealing the other marks he'd come to love, and he kissed her there, watching as she closed her eyes and the shiver he'd caused moved through her body.

"Open your eyes, baby." She lifted heavy lids, meeting his gaze. "We weren't supposed to end up here, but now that we are, I have to do the right thing because I care about you. You should be with a man who believes the fantasy. Not someone like me, who knows real life is waiting after the honeymoon period. And real life is a bitch, with bad shit coming from all sides when you least expect it."

"So it's better to let me deal with it on my own? Or with some loser who's one one-hundredth of the man you are, whose best is a half-assed job?"

She smiled up at him, and he couldn't help but return the emotion. She'd turned this around on him and exposed his Achilles' heel—*sweet, sassy, adorable, lovable, sexy, confident Amanda Jenner.*

"I think, Counselor, you are misconstruing the facts." She went up on her toes and pressed her lips to his. "I don't want you to protect me. I want you to love me."

Chapter Fourteen

ONE OF THE first things Mick had taught Amanda when she'd started working with him was never to show her hand. She'd not only shown her hand, but she'd practically shoved it down his throat—and she felt the effects in her own, as she choked on her stupidity. Lines of concentration deepened along Mick's brow. A million thoughts raced through her mind, and she was incapable of holding on to a single one.

A slow, secret smile formed on Mick's lips, only she wasn't privy to the secret. It was maddening—and irresistibly devastating.

"You're *fearless*," he said with awe.

She inhaled a breath of utter astonishment. "I am? I...I mean. I am! Of course I am." *I'm so far from fearless I can't even remember how to spell it.* "Can we pretend I never said that last part?"

"Hell no." An arrogant grin spread across his face. "But I think we can agree we've revealed enough secrets for tonight. We should let things simmer. See how we feel in the morning."

She breathed a little easier—still not easy enough, though. He hadn't responded to her confession, but he didn't tell her not to love him, either. As small as that was, she'd come to realize that it was huge in the world of Mick Bad.

"That sounds like a fair plan," she said. "I hope this won't make things awkward between us."

"I've told you things I've never told anyone, details about my sister, my father, my life. I've told you that I want you, that I want to be with you. I've revealed parts of myself I didn't even know existed." He reached for her, as if he hadn't just been a whirling tornado of emotions or that his words hadn't just sent her heart spinning again. "We know every inch of each other's bodies intimately, and you're worried about admitting you have feelings for me?"

She rolled her eyes. "Put that way, no, but...yes."

"What shall we do about that?"

"*Pfft*. Like we can do anything?"

He eyed the water. "I think I know how to wash away the awkwardness. Take your clothes off." He stepped back and began unbuttoning his shirt.

"What happened to seduction? A little foreplay?" Still reeling from all they'd said to each other, she made no move to undress.

He raised his brows and tossed his shirt on the deck, toed off his shoes, and made quick work of removing his slacks. And briefs. *And all the air from the state.* She couldn't tear her eyes away.

"Need help, or do you want to ogle a little longer?" He moved toward her with the stealth of a panther— and there was no tender underbelly in sight. His erection bobbed enticingly against his flesh. His eyes were liquid heat.

She stumbled backward. "I...No."

He took her hand and tugged her forward.

"Mick? What are we—"

In one swift move he pulled her dress over her head and tossed it aside, his expression now hovering between smoldering and playful. Cold air rushed over her skin, bringing goose bumps to her flesh. He traced a line down the center of her chest, pinched the front clasp of her bra, and flicked it open without ever looking down.

"Are you ready?" he asked in a low voice that made her belly flutter as he tossed her bra to the deck.

Despite herself, she was always ready for the excruciatingly complex and insanely intense man.

"I'm going to take that as a yes." He lifted her and guided her legs around his waist. "Don't even think about scooting down and trying to take advantage of me."

Her eyes widened. Wasn't that his intent?

"Do you know how to swim?" He stepped over the railing, and she clung to him like a monkey in full panic mode, trying to scale his shoulder to reach the deck.

"What? Yes. Wh—no! Hell no! It's going to be freezing. No, Mick. Please don't!"

His deep, hearty laugh vibrated through his chest. "Hang on, baby, because we're going down." He leaped from the boat.

"No—"

He captured her mouth just before they hit the water and sank into the frigid depths of the lake. With one arm holding her like a vise, he used the other and his powerful legs to propel them upward. They broke the surface gasping for air and laughing hysterically. He kicked and kicked, keeping their heads above the water.

"You're crazy!" She was smiling so hard her cheeks hurt. The water was freezing, but Mick's body was on fire, and she stuck to him like molten metal.

His response was another hearty laugh. Lost in the exhilarating moment, *she* silenced him with a kiss, reveling in the cold and hot sensations breaking over her skin and the hard tumbling in her chest. The kiss intensified, and they began to sink, causing her to giggle.

"What?" he said with a laugh, kicking to keep their heads above water again. "*You* kissed *me*. Everyone knows a man's brain can't function when a hot woman is wrapped around him naked. I forgot to kick." His face turned serious. "How do you feel about drowning?"

"How do you feel about getting kicked in your family jewels?"

"Not as good as I feel about drowning while making out with you." He nipped at her lower lip.

God she loved him. "I should be furious with you for making me bare my soul and—"

"Your body?"

Her head fell back and she held her fists up to the sky. "Why? Why this man, of all people?" She lowered her chin, meeting his amused expression. "No. I wanted to bare my body to you, but my soul? Not so much."

His eyes went all sad puppy on her, and she groaned. "You're hot, you're cold, you're in control, you're furious, and now this? Adorable? Are you kidding me? What's next?"

His gaze turned sinful. Pleasure radiated through her, different from the anticipatory thrill of a good fuck. This was deep-seated affection, pure, unadulterated love, filling her from the soles of her feet to the tippy top of her scalp. She wasn't fooling herself. It was a dangerous love, one he'd made clear would remain unrequited. But her brain and her heart were on different wavelengths, and no amount of intelligence could avert the emotions bedding down in her heart.

"There is no way Bridgette would have been better off without sharing the time she'd had with the man she loved—no matter how short. Memories of this weekend will last a lifetime." *They have to.* She couldn't believe she'd said it aloud, but she had, and it was the truth, and she wanted him to know it.

With a clear head and a full heart, she tried once again to abandon her hopes for more than the weekend and reveled in the luxurious experience of being with the man she loved.

**

AMANDA SHIVERED IN Mick's arms, her body pressed tightly to his, as they kissed and kissed and kissed some more, bobbing in the water like buoys. In the space of a few short days, she'd upended him like a dinghy caught in a squall—exposing fissures he'd long ago masked. With each confession the fissures expanded, until they were gaping holes, sucking him under, drowning him in emotions he didn't want to feel. Just when he thought he'd hit his limit, Amanda reeled him back to safety with a touch, a smile, a few carefully spoken words, allowing him to gain his footing and rebuild the walls. Only now they weren't quite as soundproof, not quite as thick or resilient, and Amanda was no longer standing outside those walls. She'd become a part of them.

It was those overwhelming emotions that had him guiding them toward the swim platform on the side of the yacht, because despite the heat sizzling between them, her teeth were chattering.

"Inside, baby. You're too cold." He lifted her onto the deck, and she wrapped her arms around herself as he pulled himself up, chiding himself for forgetting to toss a few towels onto the platform. He tucked her against him as they went inside, and used the control panel to close and lift the platform. "Come on. I don't want you to get sick."

In the master bedroom, Mick wrapped her in a plush robe. Holding either side of the neckline, he pulled it closed and kissed her tenderly.

"Thank you," she said through bluish lips. "I didn't realize I was this cold."

"We stayed in longer than I anticipated. Sorry, baby. Let's take a hot shower and warm you up."

Mick gathered her close, allowing the warm water to rain over her. Her arms were tucked between them, her cheek pressed to his shoulder, safely nestled in his embrace.

"That was fun," she said, teeth still chattering.

He ran his hands up and down her sides and back, trying to warm all of her at once.

She tipped her face up with a sweet smile. "Do you skinny-dip often?"

He laughed. "No. Never, in fact." She was trembling less now, warm to the touch. "Do you?"

She pressed her cheek to his chest again, wrapped her arms around his neck, and yawned. "No. Ally and I snuck into a neighbor's pool a few times when we were kids, but I haven't gone since."

"Then it's a first adult skinny-dip excursion for both of us." He kissed her shoulder, surprised by how much he liked knowing they'd shared another *first*.

They remained there, beneath the warm water, until the steam was so thick it dripped from the shower doors.

"Come on, baby, let's get you to bed." Mick dried her off and wrapped her in a dry towel before tending to himself. Amanda's lids were at half-mast, a sleepy smile on her lips. She looked delicious and sweet and so very trusting it made his heart ache and sing at once. He cradled her face in his hands and kissed her. The kiss was languid and intimate, a kiss for her tired soul to melt into.

He carried her to the bed and laid her down. She reached for him with so much love in her eyes he felt it coursing through his body, leaving her mark, claiming pieces of him he thought no one could ever reach. And he wanted more. More firsts, more time. Mornings and evenings and everything in between. He'd fought those feelings for so long, he'd truly believed he was incapable of really falling in love. But Amanda had found her way into his heart and captured nearly three years of repressed emotions as they tried to escape.

Her legs parted as he came down over her, her hips rising to greet him. He cradled her head in his hands again, overwhelmed with the love that had become too powerful to ignore.

"You're truly the most beautiful woman I have

ever seen."

"You know I'm a sure thing, right?" She playfully patted his butt.

"No. You're not a sure thing." *You're everything.* "I'm lucky to be here with you, and I meant what I said."

"Mick," she whispered, wonder washing over her features.

He kissed her softly. "You should sleep, baby. You're tired."

"I'm not too tired for our last night together."

Our last night. Like a ravenous castaway thrown into a feast, he wanted to devour every moment, every touch, every word. His emotions gorged and swelled, consuming every part of him until he ached with them.

"You're sure?"

Her smile widened. "Yes, Counselor. Stop badgering the witness."

God he loved her sassiness. His defenses were weakening to the point of transparency, and when she leaned up for a kiss, he met her halfway, deepening the kiss as their bodies joined together and they found their rhythm. Pleasure radiated through him, each thrust pulsing with the need to protect her, every kiss flooding him with the desire to cherish her. They were a perfect match in the office, in the bedroom, beneath the autumn sunlight or the evening moonlight.

He reached beneath her, angling her hips so he could take her deeper, love her more completely. Her eyes slammed shut as waves of ecstasy consumed them, pulsing around his cock as she cried out his name—and he followed her over the edge, with the pure and explosive need to love her.

They lay with their legs and bodies intertwined

like tangled vines. Awareness prickled around Mick as Amanda's heartbeat calmed and her breathing evened out. His thoughts raced forward, then retreated, pushing him in directions he never thought he'd go. She nuzzled in closer, and he kissed her cheek. *Maybe I can do this, baby. Maybe we can have a future.* Maybe he wasn't as broken as he thought.

She shifted, curling tighter against him, and a short while later, fell fast asleep in his arms.

"I love you, baby. I've loved you for a very long time," he whispered on deaf ears. That was okay, because he hadn't been sure he could actually say the words out loud. This all-consuming love terrified him, but he'd managed to say the words, and it felt incredible.

For the first time in decades, the world wasn't racing by, and Mick wasn't chasing distractions. He was exactly where he wanted to be. He drifted off to sleep with thoughts of their future dancing in his head.

Chapter Fifteen

AMANDA STOOD AT the edge of the parking lot Sunday afternoon, gazing out at the lake and wishing she and Mick could stay in this magical town forever. A cool breeze slid over her skin, and she inhaled the scent of tranquility. Funny, she hadn't felt tranquil when she'd arrived, and they'd gone through myriad emotions this weekend—a roller coaster, really. But somehow, amid all the chaos and the pretending, Amanda had found herself, and in that discovery, she'd found a sense of peace. She'd thought she needed danger and intrigue to fill the loneliness inside her, but that wasn't it at all. She'd been trying to find a substitution for the only man she really wanted. She was searching for a clone. A counterpart. A void filler. Now she knew she could have searched the world over and never would have found a man to fit the bill, because there was only one Mick Bad. And she loved him, flaws and all.

They'd spent the morning lazing aboard the boat,

and later they'd meandered through the cute shops in town. Mick bought his mother a scarf, and they ate lunch in a café. Afterward, they'd shared a cupcake from Willow's bakery and walked along the shore holding hands. Now they were packed and ready to return to the city. Or rather, packed and *nowhere near* ready to leave this little slice of paradise behind.

Mick's arms circled her waist from behind, and he pressed a kiss to her cheek. He smelled like sinful nights and sunny afternoons. He smelled like truth and trust and fear and safety, and more heavenly than any other man would again. And, she dared admit to herself, sometime between last night's conversation and this morning's lovemaking and their *favorite things* discussion that ensued afterward— his were action movies and hanging out with his brothers; hers was just about anything romantic: movies, books, proposal videos on YouTube—she'd also picked up on the faint scent of *boyfriend*.

"I really love it here." Amanda rested her head back against his shoulder. She'd slept wrapped up in him right through the night, and it had been the best sleep of her life. "I can only imagine how incredible it is as the seasons change."

"Now that you know it's here, you won't have to imagine forever." He kissed her again.

He'd been making those types of comments all morning, like near kisses that never quite connected.

"If you could go anywhere in the world," he said wistfully, "where would it be?"

She smiled, thinking of their favorite things discussion. "Greece. To a place like the resort in *Mamma Mia!* What about you?"

He laughed and reached for his phone. "Wait, I

have to add *Mamma Mia!* to my Netflix playlist."

She poked him. "I can't believe we have to leave already. It feels like we've been gone a month."

"We had a pretty perfect time, didn't we? Although, I could have done without watching you seduce another man."

"That's what we were here for." She was fishing, and not proud of it, but she couldn't help it. Mick hadn't said or done anything specific to lead her to believe they could have more than this weekend, but last night she'd felt a shift between them. And this morning, when she'd expected to wake up and realize it had all been her imagination, his eyes were warmer, less shadowed and walled off. His words were less tethered, and his touch—*God, your touch*—was possessive and dominant and somehow tender without being passive or too familiar. It could be the effects of this sweet little town, which had captured her heart and lulled her into a blissful state, but her instincts told her it wasn't the town. It was the man.

"Yes, that we were," he said with a kernel of annoyance in his tone.

She'd had a glimpse of his vulnerabilities, and they didn't lessen his virility one iota. She loved him even more for having them. They made him human. He loved his family so intensely, and she had a feeling he'd never fully grieved for the sister he'd lost far too early. It was that intensity, that passion, that made him the incredible man he'd become. He obviously saw it as a flaw, but she saw it as one of his greatest strengths. A person couldn't care *too* deeply.

She smiled, feeling the heat of the sun on her face and the tightening of his chest against her back. That was all the confirmation she needed to know he was right there with her, whether he said it or not.

"Do we really have to go back to reality?" *Reality*. It was the kind of word that carried weight, like *responsibility* and *grown-up*. The kind of word parents threw around when they were making a point.

He turned her in his arms, slid a hand to the nape of her neck, and pressed a kiss to the freckles below her ear. His eyes were full of half promises, and she held her breath, suddenly acutely aware of her quickening heartbeat and the anticipation building in her chest for the half of the promises he'd held back.

"Mick! Manda!" Louie ran across the parking lot, holding Bridgette's hand, and blew his harmonica in three long beats.

Mick turned, crouching and opening his arms seconds before Louie launched himself at him. Mick laughed as he rose to his feet and hugged the starry-eyed boy.

"There's my little man." He shifted his eyes to Bridgette. "Hey, Bridge."

"I wanted to say goodbye." Louie hugged Mick, then reached for Amanda.

Her heart squeezed as he wiggled from Mick's arms into hers and pressed his little lips to her cheek. He squirmed until he was back on the ground and ran onto the grass blowing his harmonica.

"I think that's his way of saying you should visit more often." Bridgette smiled warmly and hugged Amanda. "I'm so glad we had a chance to meet, and I hope to see you again."

"Thank you. Me too."

As Mick said goodbye to Bridgette, Amanda wondered if she *would* see them again, or if she'd let herself get caught up in the moment and made the fantasy into something it wasn't.

Half an hour later they left paradise behind and pulled onto the highway. The radio played a song Amanda had heard a thousand times, but she couldn't concentrate enough to hum along. Mick held her hand, absently stroking the spot between her finger and thumb that had given her away in the masquerade bar crawl. She realized she was waiting for him to say whatever he was about to say before they were interrupted. Apparently that ship had sailed, half promises and all.

**

MICK HAD DRIVEN slowly on the way back to the city, wanting as much time with Amanda as he could get before the real world rushed back in. It was hard to believe he'd ever thought that leaving what they'd had together behind would be easy. How could he have been such a fool? When it came to Amanda, nothing was easy. He had no idea how he could have fought his feelings for so long, day in and day out.

"Louie sure was cute, wasn't he?" she said as she unlocked the door to her apartment.

"He's something, all right."

She pushed open the door, and he followed her in, seeing her apartment for only the second time, yet somehow feeling like he'd been part of her life forever. How could one weekend feel like months?

She set her purse on the coffee table, somehow managing to look even more radiant than she had moments ago. The weekend had changed her, too. She seemed more at ease with herself, and she moved more confidently. Although, as close as they'd become, she still seemed slightly unsure around him. That didn't surprise him, though, given how fast and how far they'd come after so many mixed signals.

"I can't stop thinking about Bridgette," she said. "I know I said it last night, but I do think she was lucky to have her husband for the time she did, and she's lucky to have Louie."

He wasn't surprised that she was still thinking about Bridgette and Louie. Amanda never forgot a soul. Long after they'd closed cases, she'd bring up their clients. More often than not it was to inquire about something personal, like if he knew how the client was doing, or how the case had affected them. She had the biggest, most generous heart. It was only one of the many things that continually drew him in. He set her bag by the door and closed the distance between them.

"Yes, I think you're right." Just days earlier he might have opposed her view, but having fully opened his heart to her, he couldn't imagine how he'd ever thought any amount of time with the love of a person's life wasn't worth the pain it would cause if their lives came crashing down.

"She lost the man she loved, but he's alive in Louie, and she probably sees glimpses of him every day." She sighed and gazed out the window. "I can't wait for Heath and Ally to have kids, since I'm sure they'll have them before I do."

An icy chill ran down Mick's spine. Images of Lorelei flashed in his mind—before she fell ill, laughing as she opened a Christmas present, clinging to her bear when Mick read her one of the Goosebumps stories she loved, and then the image appeared that made his hands fist and his chest tighten. The image that made his throat close with guilt and sadness: her trusting eyes holding his while he made the promise that he'd never be able to make right.

"You want children?" How could he not have known this? He finally could see a future with Amanda. Marriage, getting old and gray together, but nowhere in that vision had he imagined children.

"Not anytime soon," she said, turning back to him. "But before I'm thirty-two or -three, I hope. I love kids, and I know I'll have to figure out my career and all of that, but I look forward to it. Family is *everything*, but you of all people know that."

"Right, family. Yes," he stammered in bewilderment as alarm bells rang out in his head. *Kids. She wants kids.*

She should have them. She should have everything.

She was saying something about when she and Ally were younger, but he was only half listening, struggling with his own conscience. Her cell phone rang, and she pulled it out of her purse.

"That's probably Ally wondering if I made it home okay."

"Take it. I'll wait." He needed the mental space anyway. He took a few steps away and paced. He pushed his hand into his pocket and pulled out the fabric pouch with the gift he'd bought for her at the festival, his heart aching anew.

She ended the call and set her phone on the table. "I told her I'd call her back." She drew in a deep breath, her shoulders lifting as her lips curved into a wide smile, and exhaled a dreamy sigh, another thing he'd come to love.

"Thank you, Mick, for the weekend, for your patience, for everything."

His love for her shoved the angst simmering inside him a little deeper. "Baby, I should be thanking you for your patience. For *your everything.*"

They both smiled with the tease.

"I got you a little something." He held out his hand and unfurled his fingers, revealing the gold fabric pouch with *La Love* embroidered on it.

Her mouth gaped. "You bought me something? You shouldn't have. You've already done so much."

Nothing will ever be enough. "This was too perfect not to buy." He placed the bag in her trembling hand and was overcome with emotion as she opened it and withdrew the necklace.

She held the gift in her palm and turned glassy eyes up to him. He lifted the necklace by the chain and turned her hand over. Her brows knitted, and she looked down at her hand as he placed the charm, a delicate gold isosceles triangle, in the space between her finger and thumb, lining up the corners to her freckles.

"A perfect match," he said, trying to ignore the ghosts and uncertainties roused by her earlier admission.

Tears slid down her cheeks. "It's so beautiful."

His throat thickened with emotion. He took a moment to wipe her tears, then put the necklace on her. He cradled her face in his hands and smiled at the woman who was changing his life, his thoughts, his beliefs, more with every second, and had now given him even more to think about.

"*You're* so beautiful. Thank you, baby, for the most incredible weekend of my life." He sealed the truth with a long, loving kiss.

"Thank—"

He silenced her with another kiss. "It was my pleasure. Think you'll be okay tomorrow?"

"Yes," she whispered.

"Okay, baby. I'll see you then."

Chapter Sixteen

MONDAY AFTERNOON MICK sat at his desk with the phone pressed to his ear and checked his watch for the fourth time since he'd taken the phone call from sports and political commentator Ben Rhapson. Mick's thirty-million-dollar lawsuit had extricated Ben from his television contract and positioned him to move to another network. They'd won the case five months ago, and against Mick's advice, Ben had gotten himself entrenched in another contractual nightmare. Normally Mick wouldn't care if the call went on for hours, but he'd been slammed from the second he'd walked into the office, and after a sleepless night, he was in desperate need of coffee.

"Ben," he interrupted his long-winded client. "Send me the docs and I'll circle back after I review them and let you know what we're looking at."

As he hung up the phone, his office door flew open and his brother Brett stepped in with a cocky grin on his face. Sophie, Mick's assistant, whom Brett loved to hit on *and* annoy, followed on his heels.

Sophie glared at Brett. She stepped in front of his very large brother, and in a professional yet firm voice said, "I told him you were on the phone."

Of the four brothers, Brett and Mick resembled each other the most, with strong, square jaws and their father's deep-set eyes. Brett also had his father's anger, and he spent hours in the gym working out the rage that seemed to simmer beneath his skin. But Brett also had a softer side, one he rarely let outsiders see, and a wicked sense of humor that rivaled his high intelligence, all of which made him an intense and complex man. Much like Mick. Brett had an inch and a good ten pounds on Mick, two things his youngest brother never allowed him to forget.

Mick shook his head. "Thanks, Soph. Brett has a hearing problem. It's called Asshole Ears."

Brett waggled his brows at Sophie. "He loves me." He flopped into a chair and patted his thigh. "Sit right down, Soph, and I'll make it up to you."

She rolled her eyes. "In your dreams."

"I usually call them fantasies," Brett said. "But if you want me to start thinking about them as dreams, I'd be happy to."

Ignoring Brett, she looked at Mick. "Conference room one—the Millers are waiting."

"Five minutes," he promised, and came around the desk.

"Seven," Brett corrected.

"Five," Mick said in his best big-brother voice, which usually was enough to buy him a few minutes before the smart-ass started in again. He waited for Sophie to close the door behind her, then crossed his arms and glowered at Brett.

"You need to cut the shit with Sophie."

"Yeah." Brett smirked. "That's gonna happen. She's tall, built, brunette, and hasn't kicked me in the balls yet. I think she digs me." Not only was Brett an ex-cop, but he and their brother Carson co-owned a multi-million-dollar security firm. He was well aware of the trouble pushing the envelope could buy him, and yet he did it at every turn.

"You're an ass." Mick had long ago stopped fighting the losing battle of getting Brett to shape up.

Brett arched a brow. "Come on, you didn't even try. *Ass?*"

"I've had a shit day." He leaned his butt against his desk and eyed his watch. "If she says I'm busy, I'm busy." His brother knew that, of course, but he also knew that short of meeting with the President of the United States, Mick would always make time for him, as he would any of their siblings.

"You don't look very busy." Brett ran an assessing eye over his brother. "In fact, you look like hell. Hm."

He'd been up half the night thinking about Amanda. Not only did his sheets smell like her, but even after changing them, his body had refused to sleep without her. He'd spent hours picking apart their weekend, his feelings, the bomb about having children she'd dropped on him last night. At three o'clock in the morning he'd finally sent her a text with a selfie of them he'd taken and the message, *Loved our secret weekend.* She'd texted back at five thirty with *Thanks for a perfect weekend. Ugh, Monday. See you soon.*

Soon turned out to be several hours later, when she'd brought a file into the conference room during a meeting. They'd locked eyes, and Mick was sure everyone in the room would have burns from the path blazing between them. She'd said, *Happy Monday, Mr. Bad,* to which he'd responded, *Thank you, Ms. Jenner.* That was the extent of their conversation. He'd excused himself from the meeting to try to catch up with her, but she'd already ducked into another conference room. He hadn't had two seconds to seek her out since.

Brett rubbed his chin. "Let's see what that could mean. A, you need to get laid, but according to Logan, that's been taken care of."

"Christ," Mick muttered. *Logan?* What the fuck?

"Which brings me to B. You're exhausted from getting laid and frustrated because...?"

Mick wasn't taking the bait until he knew how much Brett had already been told. "Logan?"

"He and I had drinks with Dylan last night. Apparently he spoke to Willow, who didn't realize Logan had no clue—like the rest of us—that you were nailing your off-limits paralegal. She talked, he listened, and shared with the rest of the class."

"Great." Mick paced. "I'm not *nailing* Amanda."

"A sexless weekend with the girl you've been pining over for years? That definitely explains why you look the way you do." Brett kicked his foot up on Mick's desk. Mick swatted it to the floor.

"I haven't been pining over anyone." Lusting, maybe, but pining was for pussies.

Brett scoffed.

"And it was anything *but* a sexless weekend."

"Then what's the issue?"

"The issue? Who said there's an issue?"

Brett rose to his feet and met Mick toe-to-toe. "Your face. Spit it out, bro, or Soph's going to come back in and you'll be forced to see me hitting on her again."

Mick laughed. "You are an ass."

"Noted. Spill."

"She's..." He glanced out the window, remembering so many moments—their intense connection across the room at the bar crawl, the way she'd looked at him when he'd revealed his identity to her Friday evening, the sweet, loving way she'd looked at him last night. He felt himself smiling, and before Brett could ride him for it, he came clean.

"She broke me, bro. I told her about Lorelei."

Brett's smirk fell, and his jaw tightened. He crossed and uncrossed his arms, the taboo subject swelling between them.

"I know," Mick said firmly. "I fucking know."

They both paced, two caged tigers circling the same demon. "And?"

"And you already know." There was no fooling any of his brothers, especially the one whose career was built on uncovering secrets and lies. For all Mick knew, Brett already knew every last detail of their weekend, including the necklace. Nah, he'd never go that far, but he could, and that was the point.

"She broke me and there's no going back."

"So, what's the issue?" Brett stopped pacing. "And don't tell me there is no issue."

Mick shrugged. "She wants kids."

"Of course she does. She's a chick," Brett said. "She's got ovaries and a uterus and hormones that make her want all sorts of things. A white picket fence. A dog. Flowers and shit."

When Mick didn't respond, Brett said, "Does she want kids now?"

"No."

"Tomorrow?"

"No."

"Next week? Next month?"

"No. Damn, Brett, cut the shit."

"This is absurd."

Mick glared at him and stalked out of his office to pace the halls. *Of course it's fucking absurd*. He stared at the path he'd worn in the carpet over the years, remembering Amanda's comment about him doing so. He wasn't about to ask her not to have children, for fuck's sake.

"They're getting antsy," Sophie said as she came up behind him.

"Two minutes. Promise." He reached for the doorknob as Amanda came around the corner. She slowed, her lips tugging up into a smile. He wanted to take her in his arms and tell her he missed her, to hold her and kiss her. But Sophie passed behind her and said, "One minute!" reminding him he was already too far behind to risk taking any longer.

He smiled at Amanda as she stepped behind him. "Hey."

"It's Monday," she said.

He noticed she had on the necklace he'd given her, and it made him warm all over. "We made it." He eyed the door. "I'm really sorry, but I'm so late—"

Her face went serious. "Of course. Go," she said, and hurried down the hall.

Mick pushed open the door, feeling like he was being pulled in a hundred directions. Brett snapped to attention, arms crossed, chin up.

"I love her," Mick said. He hadn't intended to blurt that out, but hell, it was the truth. "She's it for me. *It*. As in no other woman will ever come close." He walked around his shocked brother and gathered his files for his client meeting. "But I'm a fucked-up bastard."

"Aren't we all?" Brett came to his side, bravado and cockiness gone.

His serious, pained expression reminded Mick of the boy Brett had been before they'd lost their sister. More specifically, the look he'd had after Lorelei, the only person on earth who'd ever been able to temper the beast, had soothed his anger.

A shiver ran down Mick's spine.

"Listen, Mick. Losing Lorelei fucked us all up. No doubt about it. It sucks, and unfortunately, there's no one we can kill for taking her away. Believe me, I've tried." He said that with regret, not humor. "Dad did a job on us, or more specifically, you, but you're miles past that asshole. Now it's your turn, and you've never stood back and waited for something or someone to clear a path."

A knock sounded, and they both turned toward the door as Sophie pushed it open and peeked in. "It's been too long. They're gnawing on the conference room table. I'm afraid I'll have to install monkey bars soon."

Without missing a beat, Brett's lips curved up in a devilish grin. "I'll install them tonight; then we can try them out."

Mick glared at him.

"What? After hours, of course," Brett said.

Sophie cracked a mischievous smile that lit up her blue eyes. "Don't worry, Mick. I have a feeling Brett's all talk but no action." She closed the door behind her.

"Told you she dug me," Brett quipped.

"One day someone's going to call you on your shit

and we'll be stuck getting your ass out of jail. *Again*."
Mick pulled Brett into a manly embrace. "I love you,
man."

"You too."

"Shit, sorry. I sidetracked you. What'd you come
here for?" Mick opened the door, and they walked
toward the conference room.

"To give you shit."

Mick shook his head. His phone vibrated with a
text, and he pulled it out, cursing when their father's
name appeared on the screen.

"Have fun with that." Brett patted him on the back
and headed out of the office.

Mick opened and read the text. *Heard you signed
Pilgrim. Chip off the old block.* How his father had
already heard the news that Mick had signed Pilgrim
Entertainment less than three hours ago for what
promised to be a multi-million-dollar suit was beyond
him.

*Maybe in some ways, Pop, but not the ways that
matter.*

Before going into the meeting, he made two phone
calls, one to Logan—the big mouth—and one to
Carson, the calm, cool, and collected brother who
wouldn't give him shit.

**

AMANDA HELD HER breath as Mick's distinct footfalls,
confident, heavy, even, strode from the conference
room toward his office. He'd been in a meeting since
five with the one and only famous and stunning
actress Penelope Price. Amanda had seen her strut in
like she had one thing in mind—*seducing Mick Bad.*

She was tall, blond, and had mile-long legs men would probably pay thousands to have wrapped around their waist. *Or head. Ohgod.*

She had to stop this. Jealousy wasn't going to solve the shattering of her broken heart. It was six thirty, and she'd been trying to catch her breath since last night, when Mick had given her the beautiful necklace. She touched the delicate gold charm now, feeling a little dizzy. She'd thought the necklace symbolized their deep connection, but she couldn't have been more wrong. *Think you'll be okay tomorrow?* She'd picked apart his conflicting messages all night, and this morning she still couldn't shake the feeling that she hadn't fabricated their intense connection out of hopes and dreams alone. That was before she'd seen his text referencing their *secret weekend,* which had driven a stake into her heart. She'd shown up at work bound and determined not to make too much out of anything he did or said. She was an adult. She could handle this. Besides, she'd known exactly what she was getting into when she'd accepted his offer.

She grabbed the documents she'd printed and rose on shaky legs. It turned out she needn't have worried about misconstruing things. It would have been impossible to turn their clipped, concise, and slightly standoffish interactions into something more. Mick had obviously meant what he'd said about pretending nothing had ever happened between them—and although it shouldn't, it pissed her off, because what kind of man tells a woman he wants her, showers her with affection, shares deep, dark secrets, and then turns his back?

Adrenaline coursed through her veins as she walked toward Mick's office. The walls closed in around her, noises drowned out by the storm of blood rushing through her ears. The door to Mick's office was finally ajar. She took one long, deep breath, and pushed it open. Mick stood by the windows, tall and broad, his office filled with his manly, provocative essence and power. He turned as she closed the door behind her. In the space of a breath, her body turned to liquid—*liquid heat, liquid love*—melting her steely resolve to finally make them both face the facts. His dark brows knitted, his serious, quizzical attorney mask in place, replacing all that heat with doubt.

"Amanda?"

He didn't make a move toward her, slaying her anew, but she still refused to believe their connection wasn't real. Beneath his expensive suit, beneath his attorney facade, and despite the physical distance between them, she felt an undercurrent of love so strong it pissed her off even more that he could pretend it wasn't there, alive between them like a living, breathing soul.

"I'm not a weak, pathetic woman, Mick, and I refuse to sit back and let you make me feel..." *What? Loved?* Because despite his standing there like a statue, he made her feel loved and protected and safe and—her mind scrambled for the right words. His expression didn't change, and she was going to appear supremely weak and pathetic in about two seconds if she didn't pull her shit together.

"Like I can't read people or emotions, because I can. I did. We had something incredible and intense. We touched parts of each other—not touched, as in sexual, but—*ugh!* You know what I mean."

"Amanda—"

"Let me finish." She was breathing hard, in a full-on panic-driven tizzy, and had to get the rest out before he silenced her with his infuriatingly calm explanation of why he didn't want this to go any further.

"You can stand there cold and professional and lock away your feelings, because apparently that's something you're really good at doing. *Pretending.*" She paced, talking fast and loud—thankful the rest of the staff was mostly gone for the day—and when she realized *he* wasn't pacing, it further angered her. She had no idea what it meant that he was standing stock-still.

"I'm not buying it," she seethed. "You said you weren't scared, but you know what, Mick? I think you're terrified of allowing yourself to be happy and loved and to love someone back." She thrust the document into his hands.

He looked at the papers, his jaw tightening for the first time since she'd entered the room. *Finally.* A readable emotion.

"Is this a pleading?"

"Of course it is," she snapped. "I'm speaking your language. The one language you can't deny. Facts, legalese. The fucking smoke and mirrors you hide behind."

"Amanda," he said calmly, and shifted his eyes over her shoulder. "I can't get into this right now."

He couldn't even look at her? On the verge of angry and devastated tears, she forced herself to suck up the hurt and squared her shoulders, lifted her chin, and glared at him until he met her gaze.

"I've always known you were a lot of things, Mick, but a coward was never one of them." She spun on her heels and nearly smacked into Penelope Price.

Amanda's mind spun. The door to Mick's private bathroom was open, the light on. Mick and Penelope? How long had she been standing there? How much did she hear? Penelope's face was a mask of shock and embarrassment. Amanda mumbled an apology and fled, leaving a piece of her heart behind.

Chapter Seventeen

AMANDA FLEW THROUGH the doors of the Kiss with her heart in her throat and a whirlwind of emotions storming inside her. Dozens of annoyed customers turned and glared. The author whose reading she'd interrupted shrugged from the platform across the room. His smile was either empathetic or pitiful, she couldn't tell. She winced and mouthed, *Sorry*, then slunk to the booth where Ally was busy texting, and slid onto the seat across from her.

"Nice entrance," Ally said without looking up from her phone. Her naughty smile told Amanda she was sidetracked by whatever dirty texting game she and Heath were probably playing.

"Sorry I'm late," Amanda whispered, and flagged down the bartender, indicating an order for two more of whatever Ally was drinking. It didn't matter what it was. Gasoline would probably do the job just fine.

The efficient waiter brought the drinks quickly.

"Wait," she said, holding her finger up as she

tossed back her head and gulped down the alcohol in one swallow. Ignoring Ally's wide eyes and the amused glimmer in the waiter's, she placed the empty glass on his tray and ordered two more.

"I guess today sucked?" Ally asked.

Amanda held up a finger, trying to quell the ache in her chest before answering. She did not need to cry at the Kiss, which had become one of her favorite escapes. Romance was alive within the walls of the charming bar. Vintage lamps draped in deep burgundy and laced with intricate black flowering designs hung from the high ceiling, dangling strings of silky fringe like tiny slivers of hope. Candles were placed on rough wooden tabletops and antique furniture. Framed passages of books hung on the walls like shrines, each one lit up from below with shadowy wall sconces. Every week brave writers stood before the crowd, doling out romantic notions like food for starving hearts.

She felt Ally's hand cover hers and faced her sister's warm, empathetic expression. Amanda teared up. Her heart *had* been starving, achingly so, until the only man she'd ever loved had fed her, giving pieces of himself in glances, tender words, perfect kisses, holding and cherishing her until her heart was so full she was sure if cut, her blood would be too rich to seep out.

"Mandy," Ally whispered, causing Amanda's tears to spill down her cheeks.

Amanda grabbed a napkin and covered her face. "I promised myself I wouldn't cry!" She swiped at the unstoppable river of tears. "I told myself I wouldn't get this invested." Gulping air, she lowered the napkin and looked at Ally. "It was a weekend, an agreement, and..." Sobs stole her voice.

"Oh, honey, I'm so sorry. What happened?"

"What happened?" She half laughed, half sobbed and swiped at her tears again. "Nothing, except after three years of loving a man I never thought I could have, I had him and fell harder than I ever thought possible. So fucking hard I'd quit my job and move to the moon if it meant we could be together, and he..." She swallowed against the truth, while the other customers clapped for a reading she'd missed, and they welcomed the next author to the stage. "He was as honest and up front as he's always been. I'm an idiot."

"I wish I'd stopped you from going," Ally said. "Even though you had an *agreement*, I want to kick one of Heath's best friend's asses. And I'm totally cool with doing it, too."

Amanda shook her head, inhaling shaky breaths and forcing her tears to stop.

"No, it's not him. It's me, Al. He never lied. He never once said he loved me or said anything to make me believe we'd be anything more after our stupid Sex Adventure Weekend. And there was no mistaking the brush-off I got today, either. He didn't say more than a handful of words to me all day, and they weren't the words of lovers. They were thick black lines drawn in the carpet between the weekend and Monday."

She paused when the waiter set the drink order on the table, waiting until he walked away before she spoke again. "I tried to talk to him after work, and he said he couldn't get into it with me—right before I realized Penelope Price was standing behind me in his office in her fucking minidress and fuck-me heels with her perfect body, angelic face, and..."

Ally shook her head. "You think he's doing Penelope Price?"

"No," she admitted softly. "I don't think he's doing anyone, but it was embarrassing and shocking, and he was just so detached. It hurt, you know?" She looked down at the freckles on her hand, and more tears came.

She shoved her hand across the table and pointed to the freckles between her thumb and index finger. "See these stupid things? That's how he knew it was me that first night at the bar crawl. He noticed my freckles."

"He *noticed* your freckles?" Ally brushed her hair over her shoulders and leaned forward, studying Amanda's hand. "Those tiny things? That seems...*intimate*."

Amanda rubbed an ache at the back of her neck, remembering his affinity for all of her other freckles. "Right? Thank you. I thought I was crazy to feel like it was something special and meaningful. He'd discovered and kissed each of them—on my legs, the backs of my arms, my neck—so tenderly it felt like he was cherishing tiny diamonds embedded in my skin instead of marks I'd simply been born with."

"I can't believe he noticed something so minuscule and then treated you like that. It just doesn't make sense."

"I know," she said, feeling stronger now that she'd had a good cry. "Ally, the thing is, you know how you knew in your bones Heath was the one? You knew he loved you without a shadow of a doubt?"

"Every single day," Ally said with a smile.

"That's how I feel about Mick, like I *know* he loves me. And I know it doesn't make sense given everything else, but I do. I believe in him, and I believe in his love, and maybe that makes me a fool—"

"Mandy—"

Amanda shook her head and held up her hand. "I know. I'm a romantic fool, and I'm going to drink the crazy notion out of my head tonight, but I'm telling you, Mick loves me. He may not be ready to acknowledge it, but he does, damn it." She picked up her drink as the crowd broke into applause for the second reading she'd missed.

"Amanda."

Ally pointed over Amanda's shoulder and she turned in that direction—and spit her drink halfway across the floor at the sight of Mick standing on the platform in his dark suit and tie, with a legal pad in one hand, a bouquet of red roses in the other, and a look of love and hope in his eyes that stopped her heart. His brothers moved to and from the edge of the stage, placing vase after vase of red roses at his feet, while Heath and *his* brothers lined an aisle between her and Mick with enormous containers of white roses, spreading rose petals like a red carpet.

**

MURMURS AND WHISPERS resounded around Mick as he gazed out at the woman he'd been dying to talk to for hours. He wasn't sure his voice would work, and his heart was beating so hard he feared he might have a heart attack with the exertion it would take to speak, but that didn't stop him. Nothing would stop him from giving Amanda what she'd always dreamed of.

"Amanda." His voice cracked with emotion, and he cleared his throat. "I've faced down hundreds of corporate attorneys and legal sharks. I've won multi-million-dollar cases that took years to crack, and never in my entire life have I ever been this nervous."

The crowd laughed, and Amanda smiled, tears glistening in her gorgeous eyes.

"You gave me a legal pleading." He smiled. "You know me better than I know myself. When you came to my office this afternoon, you were so determined, so full of passion, and so relentless, it took every ounce of my willpower to keep from sweeping you off your feet. But that wasn't your dream, and I want to make all your dreams come true."

He looked at Carson, standing off to the side of the platform, an old-fashioned boom box at his feet, and he nodded. Carson grinned and pushed a button, filling the silence with "In Your Eyes" by Peter Gabriel.

Amanda's hand covered her mouth, and fresh tears tumbled down her cheeks.

"You spoke in legalese, language I know and understand. But this weekend you spoke to me in your language, the language of love and romance." He stepped off the platform and focused on the words he'd written at four o'clock this morning and had added to during his meetings this afternoon, and then he met Amanda's gaze.

"I haven't written a romance novel, and I have no passage to read. All I have is this." He held up the legal pad. "Facts. More legalese." He paused as the joke hit her and she laughed, her smile peeking out from behind her hand. He tore off a few pages and tossed the pad to the floor.

"You broke me, baby." He held up a piece of paper that read, *You set me free*, and took a step closer. Amanda was shaking, the crowd *aww*ed, and Mick's heart nearly exploded.

"You made me face my demons." He held up another piece of paper and watched as she read, *You slayed them.*

He took another step forward, and the entire room faded away. There was only him and Amanda and the pulsing air between them.

"You wanted to learn." He held up another sign, watching her tear up again as she read, *Instead, you taught me.*

He held up another sign. *About love.*

He let the papers sail to the ground and held up the next. *And life.*

And the next. *And strength.*

"Baby, I swore off having a family years ago."

Her eyes clouded over, and he took another step forward and held up another sign, then let it fall to the ground, preferring to say the words instead.

"Then came you." He closed the remaining distance between them and reached for her hand. Guiding her to her feet, he dropped to one knee and pressed a kiss to the freckles between her finger and thumb.

"I was lost, baby. And you were right. I was a coward. For almost three years I've wanted to be with you, but I was afraid of getting hurt. You deserve a full life with a real relationship. Marriage, children, a picket fence, and long, loud family vacations."

He rose to his feet, unable to stand the distance between them any longer, and slid his hand to the nape of her neck, feeling her body shiver from his touch.

"I was afraid life would come crashing down around us. Afraid I couldn't survive the pain of knowing your love and losing it. My whole life, I've been afraid of feeling, because I thought it could only lead to pain. But it turns out I never knew what pain was, because I'd never loved anyone as wholly and deeply as I love you. *Pain* is spending another night without you in my arms. *Pain* is a future without you by my side. I knew I could never live without you before we jumped off the boat and froze our naked butts off."

Amanda laughed, and it was the sweetest sound he'd ever heard.

"I have no idea if this counts as romantic, but, baby, if it's not, I'll figure it out. I promise." He reached into his pocket, withdrew a jewelry box from Tiffany's, and flipped it open.

"Mick," she whispered, drawing in several shaky breaths and clinging to his hand like he was her lifeline. Lord knew she was his.

"I've got cracks baby, but you're my glue. Let me love you, faithfully and passionately, through babies and teenagers and old age, through shit storms and magical moments and anything else life throws at us. Amanda, will you marry m—"

She leaped into his arms, her legs locked around his back, her arms around his neck, and tears flowing like a river, soaking both their cheeks.

"Yes! Yes, Mick. I'll marry you. I'll be your glue."

He sealed that promise with a kiss, and the bar erupted in applause and cheers. When their lips parted, he slid the three-carat triangle-shaped diamond ring onto her finger.

"A triangle," she said breathlessly, drawing even more love from the depths of his soul.

"Trilliant, baby. Triangle brilliant, symbolizing our

secret connection and your incredible, determined brain. You knew, you believed, and I'm one hell of a lucky man to have found such a brilliant woman."

She pressed her hands to his cheeks, smiling and crying, and searching his face.

"What are you looking for, baby?"

"The caged tiger," she said with a serious tone. "Where'd he go?"

"The only place he's ever wanted to be. In your cage—forever."

She smiled, and he tried to pull her in for another kiss before his brothers and Ally tore them apart, but she resisted.

"I thought you didn't believe in the fantasy."

"That's my girl, needing all the answers. I don't believe in the fantasy, but I believe in our reality."

He took her in another heart-pounding kiss. Their friends crowded in, cheering and teasing and pulling them apart, the way only people who loved them could. As Mick was passed from one brother to the next, his gaze never left his radiant, beaming bride-to-be, and he had only one thought—reality had never looked so perfect.

Chapter Eighteen

"ARE WE REALLY doing this?" Ally asked Amanda.

"*You* can do what you want, but me?" Amanda grinned at her sister in the bathroom mirror. "Hell *yes*. Just try to stop me." She ran her fingers over her simple white dress, fluffed her hair, and breathed deeply. It was Tuesday night. She'd been engaged for exactly twenty-four hours, and tonight she and Ally were both marrying their forever loves—at the Kiss.

"I want to do it; it's you I was worried about." Hands on hips, Ally mocked the big-sister-questioning-little-sister look Amanda had refined over the years. "You're supposed to be the careful sister."

"Careful went out the window when I bought *The Handbook*," Amanda said with a laugh. She'd stayed at Mick's last night, and they'd already made arrangements for her things to be moved into his—*their*—apartment this weekend. They'd stayed up all night talking about their hopes and dreams and their love for each other. It turned out Mick had hopes he'd never articulated, even to himself, and they all included Amanda. They'd joked about burning *The Handbook*, but neither could deny that the book had actually been instrumental in bringing them together, so they'd decided to frame it. Their inside joke, and another shared secret.

"Thank God for that stupid book," Amanda said. "If not for it, I might never have mistakenly seduced Mick."

They both laughed, and Ally's expression turned thoughtful.

"Don't look at me like that. You'll make me cry." Amanda fanned her glassy eyes. She'd been an emotional mess ever since Mick proposed. She'd experienced the strangest rivaling sensations. On the one hand, she'd been shocked, but at the same time, her heart had known all along that he was her one and only true love. The night had gotten even better when the owner of the bar, Poppy Kiss, had been so touched by Mick's proposal she'd offered to host their wedding. Mick and Amanda had exchanged one look that said a thousand words and in unison had asked, *When?* Ten minutes later the double-wedding date was set, and lucky for them, Heath had made a phone call to his family friend Treat Braden, who happened to be in town from Colorado. Treat owned resorts worldwide and had become ordained in order to marry guests. He was thrilled to host their wedding ceremony, and had even tried to talk Logan into finally tying the knot with his fiancée, Stormy, and making it a triple wedding. Logan had insisted he had wedding plans already in the works, though he refused to share any of the details.

"I'm just so happy for you," Ally said. "You've

found your *one*."

My one. Boy, did she like the sound of that.

"Mick says its kismet. Can you believe my man who doesn't believe in fantasies believes in fate? Try to figure that one out." Earlier in the day she and Mick had met with Treat to discuss the ceremony, and Treat had gushed about his wife, Max, and their children. He'd told them about how he and Max had met at his Nassau resort during a wedding, and Mick had said, *It was kismet. Like me and Amanda.* She had been floored, but then again, Mick had been blowing her away for three years.

"No, thank you," Ally said, waving her hand. "He's way too complicated for me. I'll stick with my very easy to read doctor, thank you very much." She put her arm around Amanda, both of them smiling like fools and looking in the mirror. "We're totally hot brides."

"*Brides*, Al! We're in love, getting married. I swear I need..."

They shared a knowing smile and both yelled, "Pinchigans!" as they danced around the bathroom laughing hysterically and pinching each other. The door flew open and Sophie, Mick's assistant, came in, snapping pictures on her cell phone. Ally and Amanda hammed it up, making silly faces.

"Those are totally going in the office holiday party mash-up!" Sophie leaned in for a selfie and they all stuck out their tongues. "You guys better hurry. Dylan and Brett have kicked the bartender out and have been liquoring everyone up the whole time you've been in here. Carson's eyeing Poppy like she's dinner."

Ally and Amanda exchanged a curious glance. Brett had been shamelessly hitting on Sophie all night.

"Don't even start," Sophie said, heading for the

door. "The man hits on anyone with boobs."

"She does have great boobs," Ally whispered.

Amanda giggled and grabbed Ally's hand. "I'm so nervous. What if I mess up my vows or puke? Ohmygod! What if I puke? Or pass out?"

Ally took her by the shoulders and tried to keep a serious face, but laughter burst from her lungs.

"Not helpful," Amanda said, stifling her own laugh.

"You're not going to barf, and if you pass out, Mick will catch you. Besides, we're brides; we're supposed to be nervous."

"But I'm not wearing any underwear," Amanda whispered. "Promise me if I pass out and the EMTs come, you won't let them cut my dress off, or lift it, or—"

"No time for underwear woes," Poppy said as she draped an arm around each bride and ushered them toward the back of the bar. She was like a gorgeous Martha Stewart on speed—incredibly organized, with impeccable taste and a firm but lovable hand. She had transformed the stage into a wonderland of satin and roses, lilies, and lace, and she'd even rolled out a red carpet as an aisle for the girls to walk down. She'd done it all while still running the bar. Amanda and Ally had asked her not to close the bar for the wedding. Because so many strangers had generously shared their romance with others every week, they wanted to share theirs, too.

Poppy led them to their father, who was waiting with a proud smile and tears in his eyes, the old softie. Poppy hugged them and wished them luck, then left for one last practice stroll down the aisle with their adorable flower girl, Melody, Cici and Cooper Wild's daughter.

"You are gorgeous, pumpkin," their father said to Ally, then to Amanda, "And you too, precious. I can't believe my little girls are getting married."

They both hugged him.

Jackson and Cooper were moving through the bar, taking pictures, as fluid and quiet as the moon lifted into a night sky. Cooper's camera was pointed at them, and their father pulled them in close for the shot. Amanda knew she looked more beautiful than she ever had. She felt radiant—and not just in appearance, but from her love for Mick, which she no longer tried to hold back. She knew she'd glow with that love forever.

Amanda took in the beautifully decorated stage, where their mother stood beside Mrs. Bad and Mrs. Wild, each clutching a handful of tissues. Mick's father was talking with his and Heath's brothers. Mick looked like his father, towering and stable like a California oak, but his father's eyes were dim and cold, unlike her future husband's sharp, loving gaze. She looked at her one and only, standing tall and proud and more handsome than ever. He and Heath flanked Treat, but the other men could have been stick figures or models and Amanda wouldn't have known. Her eyes found Mick's, and as usual, the rest of the world faded away.

**

THE BAR HAD filled with people during the ceremony, but while Mick was aware of their presence, his thoughts were focused on the woman talking with his mother a few feet away. Amanda's eyes had brimmed with light as they'd recited their vows. She looked happy, wise, and beyond beautiful. She looked like a woman in love, and knowing she was in love with *him* brought a sense of pride and responsibility Mick gladly accepted.

"The hot blonde at the bar said to tell you congratulations," Dylan said as he came to Mick's side.

He glanced over and nodded at his client Tiffany Winters, wondering what the hell she was doing there.

"How do you know her?" Dylan asked.

"Client," Mick said, sensing the interest in his brother's tone. "She's a cutthroat sports agent. Stop looking at her like she's sex on legs. She'll eat you alive, Dyl."

Dylan scoffed, eyeing the blonde. "What makes you think that?"

"You have a thing for needy women. You're a savior, and she wouldn't let a man help her if she was hanging on to the edge of a cliff and he was her only hope."

"Why does that turn me on?" Dylan said with a smirk.

Mick shook his head as Dylan walked toward the claws that would surely tear him to shreds. The man must have a death wish. *Not my problem.*

Their father stepped into Mick's line of sight, blocking his view of his wife. Damn, he liked the sound of that. *My wife.*

It had been a long time since he'd seen his parents in the same room, and he hadn't been sure how tonight would go. He watched his father making his way toward him. There had been a time when Mick had seen him as all-powerful, even untouchable, but that was so long ago and buried so deeply under the visceral anger that consumed him every time he thought of the man, he had a hard time conjuring up those memories. They felt more like a story he'd been told. *There was once a man...*

Mick took a drink as his father came to his side. He bit back the distaste of the past and vowed not to allow it to eat away at his future. He had a wife now, a woman he adored, and one day they hoped to have a family. *A family*. Their family. He spent so much time afraid of the thought, and now all he wanted was to revel in it with Amanda.

Until now, when the very presence of the man standing shoulder to shoulder with him made his blood boil, opening the door to the ghosts of their past. As they stared out at the crowd—instead of at each other—Mick wondered if his father ever tired of carrying around the weight of their familial destruction. He sure as hell did.

"How does it feel?" his father asked.

"Different." Mick finished his drink and set the glass on the table beside him.

"Better?" he asked, without looking at Mick.

Mick turned his head and took in the rugged and somber profile of the man who was too weak to pull his shit together for his family. The man who'd spent fourteen years pushing him to be the best person he could be—and in two short years made him fear the man he could become.

His father lifted his glass and met his gaze. The jet-black hair they'd once had in common was now layered with silver, magnifying the inky blackness of his deep-set eyes. His square jaw visibly tensed, deepening the etched markings of his shadowy past.

"I don't know, Dad. Is it?" The question came unbidden, and as his father's eyes narrowed, he knew he understood the question had nothing to do with his recent nuptials. A long, silent moment stretched between them, each stubborn man holding his ground. Mick was no longer sixteen years old, frightened and fighting to hold their family together. The rest of them had made it and remained willing to lay their lives on the line for one another, but Mick had absolutely no clue where that left his father.

His father's lips curved up at the edges in a hint of a smile, stopping short of coming to fruition. It was the smile of a pleased mentor and the smile of a man who knew better than to show his hand.

"No," his father answered.

Mick swallowed hard at the unexpected response.

"Nothing has, or will ever be." His father lifted his drink, watching his son as he swallowed it down. "For me, that is." He looked out over the crowd. "But I sure as hell hope it will be for you."

Anger burned up Mick's chest. Dylan lifted a glass, catching his attention and sparking thunderous memories of that fateful, stormy night. He and Carson were heading toward them. Brett, watching the troops rally, fell into step behind the others while their mother watched with pride and hurt in her eyes. She was a strong woman, and she'd built a life around what she had, not whom she'd lost. They were happy despite their scars, each pushing through their own silent battles. Each brother there to help the others. Comrades, confidants, and friends. They'd made it despite their father's fall. They all had.

"It could have been better for you," Mick challenged his father. "But you chose to throw it away."

His father drew in a deep breath, his jaw tight, eyes unflinching. "Devastation isn't a choice, son." He turned with a rueful expression that cut Mick to his core. "Not a day passes that I don't wish I'd been stronger."

His brothers' faces grew serious as they approached.

"Me too," Mick said honestly. He wished his father had been stronger, and he wished he'd been stronger, too.

Dylan, the peacemaker, inserted himself between the two of them. Carson, his strong, silent brother who had the strength of ten men—emotionally and physically, though an onlooker would never think it, given his easy demeanor—took up the space on Mick's other side. Brett stood before them, arms crossed, the unyielding corner pin rounding out the group.

Mick looked past Brett, to his new wife, and realized his group, his cavalry, had expanded, as had his charge. He'd become the patriarch of his small family. Amanda turned, and the space between them sparked and hummed. Love was a powerful thing, and Mick knew in his heart he'd never lose sight of that. He was stronger with her by his side, and if life brought a shit storm, he'd shelter her. If life brought pain, he'd nurse her through it. But he'd never in a million years allow his weakness to overpower their love. His father was right. Devastation wasn't a choice, but how a person treated the people they loved was.

Dylan looked over his shoulder at Amanda and smiled at Mick. "You going to stare at her all night?"

"No," Mick said, holding his hand out to his wife and pulling her in close. "I'm going to stare at her for the rest of my life."

Want More After Dark Romance?
Check out the rest of the series

WILD BOYS AFTER DARK

Wild Boys After Dark: Logan
Wild Boys After Dark: Heath
Wild Boys After Dark: Jackson
Wild Boys After Dark: Cooper

BAD BOYS AFTER DARK

Bad Boys After Dark: Mick
Bad Boys After Dark: Dylan
Bad Boys After Dark: Brett
Bad Boys After Dark: Carson

Each of Mick's siblings will have their own books. Are you ready for Dylan Bad?

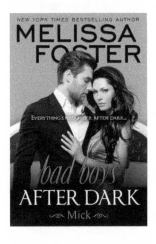

Sinfully sexy bar owner Dylan Bad has a thing for needy women. He's a savior, a knight in shining armor, and his mighty talented sword has no trouble bringing damsels in distress to their knees. Enter Tiffany Winters, a gorgeous cutthroat sports agent who looks like sex on legs, fucks like she's passion personified, and wouldn't let a man help her if she was hanging onto a ledge and he was her only hope. One night and too much tequila might change their lives forever. The question is, will either one survive?

Fall in love with Trish & Boone
Chased by Love (The Ryders)

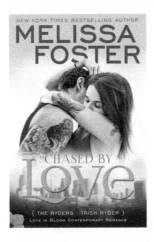

"I'M GOING OVER. Should I go over? Tell me I shouldn't. Or should I?" Trish Ryder clutched her cell phone, pacing inside her trailer on the set of her latest film, *No Strings*. She'd been trying to study her lines all night, but her costar, famed rocker Boone Stryker, had a full-blown party going on at his trailer, and she could barely think past the noise.

"It's midnight and you have to be on set in seven hours," her best friend, Fiona, reminded her. "*You're* the star, so yes. Get your ass over there and pull a diva."

Trish stopped cold. "But I'm *not* a diva!"

"Of course not, but you know that's what his groupies will think, which you do *not* care about. Right?"

"Right." She nodded curtly, but she *did* care. She cared a lot, and Fiona knew that about her. She'd worked hard to keep a professional reputation clear of any diva attitude or impressions, and she didn't want to blow it for a self-centered rock star making his film debut.

Fiona groaned, and Trish heard her friend's fiancé, Jake Braden, say, "Give me the phone."

"Do *not* give him the phone." Trish paced again. She adored Jake. Not only was he an amazing stuntman, but he treated her bestie like a princess. But Jake, like each of Trish's five brothers, had the protective alpha thing down pat, which meant he'd want to take care of this *for* her.

"Like I have a choice?" Fiona giggled, and Trish heard them struggling over the phone.

"Trish?" Jake's tone made her name sound like a command she should salute.

Trish Ryder saluted no man. "No, it's Mary Poppins."

"Okay. Well, listen, Mary," Jake said without missing a beat. "March your pretty little ass over there and tell the guy to straighten up. If he gives you any crap, call me back, and I'll come to the set and knock some sense into him."

Of course you will. "Thanks, Jake, but I can handle it. I just wasn't sure I wanted to stir up trouble. He's already messed up so badly, the whole crew knows the film's on thin ice."

"Even more of a reason for you to set him straight," Jake said. "You don't have to be a bitch. Just be your normal, confident self. He'd have to be a real dick not to rectify the situation."

She sighed, and heard Jake pass the phone back to Fiona. Maybe they were right. She was a well-respected actress, and this *was* Boone's first film. Maybe he simply wasn't up to speed on film-set etiquette. Obviously, since in the span of a few weeks he'd missed the preproduction meeting, showed up late to the set, and screwed up too many scenes to count.

"I'm back. You okay?" Fiona asked.

"Yes. No. I don't know, but I'm going over. You guys are right. If I'm awake all night, I'll be the one messing up tomorrow, and I don't need the director upset with me."

After Trish ended the call, she set her phone down beside a copy of *Rolling Stone* magazine. A picture of Boone, shirtless, graced the cover. She'd read the article. She'd read every article about Boone taking on the role in *No Strings*, and they all said the same thing. *Boone Stryker is everything fantasies are made of: warm brown eyes that say "help me," "do me and you'll never forget me," body ink indicative of a troubled soul, and an insurmountable dedication to his craft.*

They left out *self-centered asshole with no respect for anyone but himself.* And based on his behavior, she wasn't even sure he had that.

Well, guess what? It's time to grow up.

Her phone vibrated with a call from her eldest brother, Duke. She groaned. *Damn it, Jake. You've got a big freaking mouth.* Sometimes being a little sister sucked—even at almost thirty years old. She let the call go to voicemail. She wasn't in the mood to deal with her overprotective eldest brother who was ten years her senior. When would he learn that having ovaries didn't mean she needed looking after?

She stormed out of her trailer, assaulted by the sounds of rock and roll coming from across the lot. Groups of scantily clad women and shirtless men, smoking and drinking, created a buffer between Boone's trailer and the rest of the world. Trish stood and watched for a moment, trying to spot Boone among the mass of swaying bodies. She couldn't imagine living with groupies around all the time. It was no wonder he showed up late and was never prepared. How could anyone deal with this and concentrate on anything?

She tossed her hair over her shoulder and lifted her chin, squaring her shoulders like she wasn't nervous at all. She was an actress. She could do this, and Jake was right. There was no need to be a bitch. She'd act calm and cool, and hopefully Boone would respond reasonably. *Cool. Yeah, right.* She didn't usually have trouble with confrontations, but the badass rocker struck chords she'd never had tweaked before, and he did it with little more than a glance, which was horribly embarrassing. She couldn't deny the rush of heat that consumed her every time their eyes connected. Unfortunately, as hot as their chemistry was off set, when she and Boone were acting, he became cold, like he didn't want to feel the heat. In an effort to keep the situation from becoming even more uncomfortable, she'd kept her distance when they were off set. She hated that this would be their first *real* interaction. But that was on him, she decided, and set out across the lot, hoping to get this over with as quickly as possible.

The smell of cigarettes, weed, sweat, and sex hung heavily in the air. She pulled her arms in close, turning sideways to fit between less-than-accommodating people, and weaved through the drunken mob toward his trailer. She scanned the crowd for Boone, trying to ignore the way men and women were eyeing her up. She was used to being looked at, and she wasn't generally judgmental, but the groupie vibe and raunchy smell made her feel like she needed a shower. Stat!

"Hey, babe," a long-haired guy said as she squeezed between him and a busty brunette.

She forced a smile and pushed past, making a beeline for the trailer door. It seemed ridiculous to knock, given the scene she'd just waded through, but she knocked anyway. No one answered. She knocked again, louder, and when no one answered, she tried the knob. Locked. *Perfect*. The asshole was probably passed out naked with a harem of women. An icy chill rushed down her spine. *Yuck*. She pushed her way back through the crowd, determined to give him hell tomorrow, regardless of how it affected the movie. This was bullshit. How could he sleep with all that racket?

"Trish?"

She startled at the sound of Boone's voice coming from the direction of the parking lot and spun around. He had the most sensual voice she'd ever heard. It didn't matter if he was singing or acting, it affected her every time. It was deep and rich, and somehow rough, demanding both attention and intimacy. She tried to steady her racing heart with a few deep breaths as she drank him in. He held his guitar case in one hand and sported a half-cocked smile. He had beautiful full lips, and despite everything, the mere sight of his perfectly bowed mouth made hers water. His faded T-shirt clung to every muscle in his insanely defined chest. Lust chased frustration up her body. She had the inside scoop on his selfishness and *still* she wanted to fell him like a tree and devour him limb by perfect limb.

She swallowed a puddle of drool, drew her

shoulders back again, and set a hand on her hip, hoping to mask her attraction. His smile turned smug, and his eyes lit with a spark of intel that made her gut twist. *Bastard.*

"Did I wake you?" She might not have been able to mask her attraction, but every word she spoke was laden with sarcasm.

He ran a hand through his hair and sighed, as if he were bored with the conversation. Or maybe with life.

"Wake me?" he said with an arched brow. "I just got here."

She glanced at the crowd and pointed to her ears, indicating the blaring music there was no way he could miss, and glared at him. "You just let your groupies run wild like this while you're not even around?"

He strode toward her, his piercing dark eyes sucking her right into his vortex. He stopped when they were toe to toe, filling the air with his confident arrogance and making it hard to breathe, much less concentrate.

"I had no idea they were partying. I'll shut it down. But for the record, no. I don't let my *groupies* run wild." His gaze roved over her face, and she narrowed her eyes, hoping he couldn't see the way every sweep sent waves of heat to all her best parts. "You went over there?"

"Some of us take this movie seriously. I can't prepare with that noise going on all night."

Boone raked his eyes down her body, causing her to nearly combust. A sinful smile curved his lips as his eyes began a slow stroll north, over her hips, lingering on her breasts, and bringing her traitorous nipples to attention, greeting him like a long-lost lover.

"Pretty woman like you shouldn't scowl so much." His rich voice slid over her skin like a caress, leaving goose bumps in its wake.

God, she hated herself right now.

Unwilling to give him the upper hand, she flashed a haughty smirk and returned his assessment with a lecherous leer of her own, drinking in every inch of his athletic build, from his bulging biceps to the ripped abs evident beneath his clingy shirt, all the way to the formidable package at the juncture of his powerful thighs. She lingered there, brazenly licking her lips.

He leaned in close—so close she thought he might kiss her. And damn it to hell, she wanted him to. Lust and challenge pulsed between them, thick and alive like a third heart. She shifted her eyes away and noticed a gorgeous platinum blonde standing in the shadows behind him. Embarrassment and something that felt far too similar to the claws of jealousy dug into her.

Her eyes shot to Boone, but before she could say a word, he said, "I'll take care of the noise," and stalked away with an arm around the blonde.

—End of Sneak Peek—
**To continue reading, purchase
CHASED BY LOVE (The Ryders)**

Meet Grayson Lacroux
Your next book boyfriend

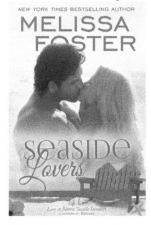

PARKER COLLINS SHOVED a handful of M&M's in her mouth, eyes glued to *Saw III.* A burst of light illuminated the pitch-black media room, followed by a scream of terror. Christmas, her four-year-old English mastiff, sacked out beside her on the couch, pushed his big head beneath her legs as darkness shrouded them again. Another shrill scream brought her big chicken of a dog deeper into her leg tunnel.

"Whoever said dogs were a *man's* best friend was an idiot. *My* best friend." *Especially now that Bert's gone.* A few tears slipped down her cheek.

Christmas whimpered, pulled his head from beneath her legs, and licked her from chin to eyes, getting every last one of her tears and coming back for more. He'd been lapping up her tears for two weeks, ever since she'd lost her friend, mentor, and the only family she'd ever known. Bert Stein had suffered a massive heart attack while Parker was in Italy filming her latest movie, and she'd been moving on autopilot ever since: picking up Christmas from his housekeeper in Los Angeles because Bert had been watching him while she was away, attending Bert's funeral, *trying to remember how to breathe*, and finally, coming to her house in Wellfleet to mourn—and, she hoped, to mend a fence Bert was never able to with his estranged brother.

Holing up in the bay-front home she'd built for the Collins Children's Foundation, where no one would look for her, was the only way she could grieve without negative ramifications. God forbid an A-list actress went out looking like an average woman whose heart had been ripped from her chest. Rag magazines would pay big bucks for pictures of her puffy, tired eyes and I-don't-give-a-shit tangled hair. She could just imagine the headlines: *Parker Collins's New Drug Addiction,* or *Unplanned Pregnancy for Parker,* or anything else that would sell magazines. Nobody cared that she'd never even smoked a cigarette, that she needed to have sex in order to get pregnant, or that she'd gone so long without, she wondered if her best parts even worked anymore.

She pressed her hands to Christmas's droopy cheeks, kissed her bewildered boy's snout, and reached for the bottle of tequila she'd been nursing. She'd never had tequila before tonight, but it was the perfect addition to her chocolate–horror movie grief remedy. After pouring herself another shot, she tossed it back in one gulp, savoring the warmth as it slid down her throat and drowned her sadness.

She set the glass beside her on the couch and shoved her hand into the jumbo bag of peanut M&M's that had consoled her throughout the evening— because a big lazy dog was great for licking tears, but nothing quenched sadness like candy-coated chocolate. And tequila. *Definitely tequila.* Her fingers scraped the bottom of the bag. *Damn it.* She tossed the empty bag to the floor. Christmas hung his head over the side of the couch and whimpered.

"Don't judge me. It can't be that bad." She leaned forward to assess the damage, knocking an empty pizza box to the floor, and reached for the coffee table to stop the room from spinning. "Whoa."

Another scream brought her eyes to the movie, then toward the movement in her peripheral vision, where a shadowy figure blocked the entrance to the media room. It took her alcohol-drenched mind a minute to realize the tall, broad man filling the doorway wasn't supposed to be in her house. Panic spread through her veins, catapulting her to her feet. Christmas darted to the stranger with a friendly *woof.*

"Oh God." She reached for the wall to steady the spinning room, fighting to push through her drunken haze. She'd seen enough movies to know she was going to die in the media room of this lonely house, wearing chocolate-stained sweatpants—or more accurately, ice-cream-, tequila-, pizza-sauce-, *and* chocolate-stained sweatpants—while her dog made a new friend of her killer.

"Stay back. He's a killer. One command and you're dead!" Not likely with her loving dog.

The man sank to one knee, his face hidden by her big, traitorous dog.

"Yeah, I can see that," he said casually, as only a coldhearted psycho killer could.

Searching for a weapon, she grabbed the tequila bottle, only too late realizing it was spilling down her wrist. She flipped it upright, wishing this was a movie and someone would yell, *Cut!*

A piercing scream drew their attention to the heart-pounding terror on the projection screen. Suddenly the room was showered in light. Parker's eyes slammed shut against the sensory invasion, then flew open to get a look at the man who would probably find fame as the *Parker Collins Killer*.

Her breath caught in her throat, and her hand flew to her frantically beating heart, as she took in the Greek god rising to his feet before her. His smoldering dark eyes nearly brought her to her knees. *Grayson Lacroux.*

"Grayson?" *Do I sound scared, drunk, or like I want to jump your bones?* Probably all three, which wasn't good. Grayson had won a two-year contract in a design competition last summer, and for the past ten months he'd been designing artwork for the Collins Children's Foundation. As the founder of CCF, Parker headed up the project, and they'd exchanged hundreds of emails—emails that felt intimate and meaningful and had pulled her through too many long, lonely nights to count.

"What are you doing here?" She cringed at how breathless she sounded. Even in her drunken state she knew it had nothing to do with her initial fears and everything to do with the towering male across the room.

His lips curved up as he surveyed the room. She'd come straight down to the media room in full-on holing-up mode after arriving from LA. Her open suitcase lay in the middle of the floor, lace and silk seeping over the sides. The clothes she'd worn on the flight were strewn across the hardwood floor. One pink high heel peeked out from beneath an empty bag of Twizzlers; the other was nowhere in sight. An orgy of fun-size candy bar wrappers and M&M's littered the floor.

"I might ask you the same thing." His voice was low and rich and made the room feel fifty degrees hotter.

Maybe that's the tequila.

"I came to take measurements for the railing and heard a noise. I didn't know you were here."

Measurements? She couldn't think with his dark, assessing gaze trained on her as he crossed the room. Each step was a declaration of power and control—the same air of confidence he relayed in his emails. Parker was used to beautiful people, but holy mother of hot and sexy men, Grayson brought manliness and sex appeal to a whole new level. An *enticingly tempting* level. She was five nine, and he had several delicious inches on her. His bulbous biceps and massive breadth made her feel more delicate than she was. His tousled, thick dark hair and unwavering air of command made her knees wobble. She took a deep, unsteady breath and backed against the wall to stabilize those wobbly knees, but he stepped closer, assaulting her senses with his musky, and somehow summery, scent.

Nope. Definitely not the tequila. The man was a walking heat wave.

He eyed the tequila bottle in her hand, and his eyes filled with amusement. "Having a little party?" He plucked a sticky piece of candy from her hair and held it between his large finger and thumb with a cocky grin.

A crazy-hot cocky grin that sent dirty thoughts about his mouth rushing to the front of her mind. "Not exactly," she mumbled.

"You've been avoiding my emails."

She'd been avoiding email, voicemail, and *life* since Bert's funeral. Grayson was on her callback list, along with her agent, a few foundation staff members, and about a dozen so-called friends.

"I...Um..." *Can't really think clearly.* She lifted the tequila bottle. "Care to join me?"

His gaze dragged down her tank top, bringing her nipples to attention and reminding her she'd taken off her bra. As if on cue, Christmas *woofed*, Parker's pink lace bra dangling from his mouth. Grayson's eyes brimmed with heat, making her want to put him on a totally different kind of *to-do* list.

He'd been the subject of her late-night fantasies for so many months she felt like she already knew him well enough for him to own that list.

This was bad.

Very, very bad.

Parker didn't have that kind of *to-do* list. She *did* relationships. Or rather, *didn't* do them, based on her dating history.

Ugh! Her head was too fuzzy to try to untangle the web of lust she'd weaved with every email, every intimate glance into his private world of family, friends, and his love of his craft. Grayson worked with heavy metals, as evident from his insanely perfect physique, which no gym in the world could produce, and his designs were excruciatingly unique and beautiful. Parker had probably driven him crazy making changes, but if she had, he'd never let on. She loved reading his descriptions about why he designed certain pieces and how he felt when he was creating them. Sometimes he wrote about missing his family, or about bonfires and outings he'd gone on when he flew home to work with his brother on specific designs for

CCF. She'd been careful not to ask personal questions, so she wouldn't feel inclined to share her personal life, but she had secretly clung to each of his tales, treasuring the emotions he so eloquently shared. She'd made excessive design changes just to keep those intimate glances of him coming.

And now he was here, all six-something feet of him, close enough to see and touch and taste—and between her grief and his godliness, she was clearly losing her mind.

She pushed past him, grabbed the lingerie from Christmas, and tossed it into her suitcase. "Lie down."

Christmas walked in a circle and plopped onto a pile of clothes with a huff.

Parker grabbed a shot glass from the bar, determined to remain in her inebriated state so she could deal with all the testosterone flinging around the room, and sank down to the couch. "Coming, big guy?"

—End of Sneak Peek—
**To continue reading, purchase
SEASIDE LOVERS (Seaside Summers)**

More Books By Melissa
"Contemporary romance at its finest"

LOVE IN BLOOM SERIES

SNOW SISTERS
Sisters in Love
Sisters in Bloom
Sisters in White

THE BRADENS
Lovers at Heart
Destined for Love
Friendship on Fire
Sea of Love
Bursting with Love
Hearts at Play
Taken by Love
Fated for Love
Romancing My Love
Flirting with Love
Dreaming of Love
Crashing into Love
Healed by Love
Surrender My Love
River of Love
Crushing on Love
Whisper of Love
Thrill of Love

THE BRADENS – NOVELLAS
Promise My Love
Daring Her Love

THE REMINGTONS
Game of Love

Melissa Foster

Stroke of Love
Flames of Love
Slope of Love
Read, Write, Love

SEASIDE SUMMERS

Seaside Dreams
Seaside Hearts
Seaside Sunsets
Seaside Secrets
Seaside Nights
Seaside Embrace
Seaside Lovers
Seaside Whispers

The RYDERS

Seized by Love
Claimed by Love
Chased by Love
Rescued by Love
Thrill of Love

AFTER DARK SERIES
WILD BOYS

Logan
Heath
Jackson
Cooper

BAD BOYS

Mick
Dylan
Carson
Brett

NICE GIRLS

Phoebe
Francine

Bad Boys - Mick

Nicole
Genevieve

HARBORSIDE NIGHTS SERIES
Includes characters from
Love in Bloom series

Catching Cassidy
Discovering Delilah
Tempting Tristan
Chasing Charley
Breaking Brandon
Embracing Evan
Reaching Rusty
Loving Livi

More Books by Melissa
Chasing Amanda (mystery/suspense)
Come Back to Me (mystery/suspense)
Have No Shame (historical fiction/romance)
Love, Lies & Mystery (3-book bundle)
Megan's Way (literary fiction)
Traces of Kara (psychological thriller)
Where Petals Fall (suspense)

Melissa Foster

Sign up for Melissa's newsletter to stay up to date with new releases, giveaways, and events

NEWSLETTER:
www.melissafoster.com/newsletter

CONNECT WITH MELISSA

TWITTER:
www.twitter.com/Melissa_Foster

FACEBOOK:
www.facebook.com/MelissaFosterAuthor

WEBSITE:
www.melissafoster.com

STREET TEAM:
www.facebook.com/groups/melissafosterfans

Acknowledgments

I'd like to give a special shout-out to Alexis Bruce for our fun chats about our dirty boy, Mick Bad, and heaps of gratitude to all my fans and readers for sharing my books with your friends, chatting with me on social media, and sending me emails. You inspire me on a daily basis, and I can't imagine writing without our interactions. Some of you have even had characters named after you, which is always so much fun for me. Thank you for sharing yourselves with me.

If you don't yet follow me on Facebook, please do! We have such fun chatting about our lovable heroes and sassy heroines, and I always try to keep fans abreast of what's going on in our fictional boyfriends' worlds.
http://www.Facebook.com/MelissaFosterAuthor

Remember to sign up for my newsletter to keep up to date with new releases and special promotions and events and to receive an exclusive short story that was written just for my newsletter fans about Jack Remington and Savannah Braden.
http://www.MelissaFoster.com/Newsletter

For a family tree, publication schedules, series checklists, and more, please visit the special Reader Goodies page that I've set up for you!
http://www.MelissaFoster.com/Reader-Goodies

As always, heaps of gratitude to my amazing team of editors and proofreaders: Kristen Weber, Penina Lopez, Jenna Bagnini, Juliette Hill, Marlene Engel, Lynn Mullan, and Justinn Harrison.

~Meet Melissa~

Melissa Foster is a *New York Times* and *USA Today* bestselling and award-winning author. Her books have been recommended by *USA Today's* book blog, *Hagerstown* magazine, *The Patriot*, and several other print venues. She is the founder of the World Literary Café and Fostering Success. Melissa also hosts Aspiring Authors contests for children and has painted and donated several murals to the Hospital for Sick Children in Washington, DC.

Visit Melissa on her website or chat with her on social media. Melissa enjoys discussing her books with book clubs and reader groups and welcomes an invitation to your event.

Melissa's books are available through most online retailers in paperback and digital formats.

CPSIA information can be obtained
at www.ICGtesting.com
Printed in the USA
LVHW09s0618190818
586752LV00003B/193/P

9 781941 480403